dogged STAR 

a novella

for Sarah & David

'DOGGED STAR'   **ISBN 978-1-7750471-7-9**

DISCLAIMER: *'DOGGED STAR' is a work of fiction inspired by the fifteenth-century studio painting of 'Tobias and the Angel', the pages of Leonardo da Vinci's notebooks, hearsay, and snippets and anecdotes from historical documents.*

SILENT K PUBLISHING
Vancouver Island, British Columbia, Canada

TABLE OF CONTENTS

1

MILADY UNIVERSE

2

SIGHT UNSEEN

3

FINDHORN FEVER

4

PAINTING 101

5

TOBIAS and the ANGEL

6

BED UNREST

7

MATERNAL DYSFUNCTION

8

AMAZING FACE

9

VESPERS

10

SARAH & ME

11

OBEDIENCE SCHOOL

12
NO END IN SIGHT

13
THE DARKEST HOUR

14
SATORI

15
TIME OF DEATH

16
FIRENZE

17
DÉJÀ VU AGAIN

18
THE DREAM

19
CLEAR SIGHTED

20
SARAH'S SECRET

The Denouement
DOGMATIC TO THE END

'TOBIAS & THE ANGEL' - c.1468

The Dog Days of Summer,
named for the sweltering weather
that coincides with the year's
heliacal rising of Sirius, the Dog Star,
begins July 3 and officially ends
on August 11th

CHAPTER 1 - **MILADY UNIVERSE**

'Vincent' - Don McLean

JULY 3, 2022

THE 'DOG DAYS OF SUMMER' BEGIN

Once upon an ominous star, a dog was born. By my reckoning we were hapless twins born 500 years apart. I presume such a wild notion because the universe creates wondrous paradoxes in plain sight, which is why a tail can wag a dog, a human can dream a lifetime in the space of a cat nap, and unexplained phenomenon can doggedly serve humans in unimaginably perverse ways.

Case in point. My eyes have six months to live. Tragic for a photographer, ruination for a painter of fine miniatures, and damnably inconvenient for an art historian editing their first book.

Unfortunately, the only upshot of perpetual head-on collisions with disaster is that serious challenges come as no surprise. I'd been expecting a long overdue catastrophe for thirty-three years -- ever since I turned nineteen.

Many years after the catastrophe, hindsight offered me the ability to see forever. And so, from my future proverbial mountaintop, I offer you a constructive warning regarding the darker side of astrophysics: Astrology can be dangerous to your psychic health.

The premise that a desperate seeker will involuntarily progress through a mystical life dictated by precisely plotted degrees, condemned to house-hopping in a dangerous celestial neighborhood, is unconscionable.

I can state unequivocally that possessed tealeaves under the paranormal influence of cosmic geometry will never gravitate to the inside of a seeker's teacup, neither will a life sentence of being regularly evicted from haunted *houses* in a nonlocal housing estate of mythical latitude and longitude, bring sustainable peace and prosperity. Wandering aimlessly under the presumed identity of an unstable sun sign will never result in a conscious authentic life.

For sure and certain, when crystal balls, tea leaves, and tarot cards collide, a grumpy Bermuda triangle of spiritual alchemy manifests to do its worst. Like the moon rising in a fictional house of chaos, it will wreak havoc.

Sadly however, humanity's collective unconscious is programmed to pollute the waters of the purest mountain stream into toxic waste, and it's easy to confuse the voices in your head. But this I do know: superstition is the breeding ground for mystical *'focus pocus'*. Back away slowly from naysayers, soothsayers, and witches selling apples. And talk yourself down from the ledges where you find yourself most bewitched by fear.

The face in your looking glass never lies. It's called a reflection for a reason. You are an oracle.

The subtleties of cosmic dynamics are a hornet's nest of science and fiction. However, in the spirit of forewarned being forearmed, it has been my experience with the paranormal that beyond the stars there be dragons. Dragons and ghosts in all shapes and disguises, both ethereal and metaphorical. Many many ghosts!

Shakespeare said it best. *"There are more things in heaven and earth, Horatio, than are dreamt of in your philosophy."*

Game changers may save the day in the 'all is lost' beats of movie magic but offscreen life proves there are a limited number of pots of anything at the ends of rainbows. Silver linings are the things of mythology. I once classified them as irrational thinking. And if that wasn't challenge enough, I made it my life's purpose to learn everything the hard way.

I bought a losing ticket in a celestial lottery, once. As I recall it was bit of a mug's game. To win the jackpot one required blind faith in a higher world. But tragically, the mystical kismet I briefly held dear had long since drifted out to sea and fallen off the horizon. My world shrank pancake flat and oppressively routine, and luck had nothing to do with Shakespeare's lofty *'what dreams may come'* wisdom. With one exception, every dream that came for me, shattered.

And yet, setting the divine's wicked sense of humor aside, I'd been known to wax philosophical from time-to-time, so, it was not lost on me that my present predicament was not too shabby an irony for an aging visionary in a fervent quest for fresh insight.

I've heard that moments of genius appear out-of-the-blue, my latest being an intuitive nonsensical newsflash that the all-seeing universe was inherently female the day I had my eyes tested for new spectacles.

I'd had a prolonged season of killer headaches. It was time for a prescription update. Stronger lenses. No big deal. Then came the diagnosis and I had an epiphany: Maybe *everything* comes out of the blue!

Clearly, I was manifesting the wrong shade of blue. Indigo is not the color of joy; it's the nearest color to the frigid void of outer space where stars are born to trine, oppose, and subdue mankind into cave dwellers of limited imagination.

A miniscule tumor pressing on my optic nerve was discovered early. 'I was lucky,' the doctors said. There was every chance for a full recovery after a relatively routine minor surgery. Perhaps a short aftermath of impaired vision but nothing more. With advances in optical science, not to mention the last resort of a state-of-the-art seeing-eye dog, I would likely cope with walks in the park in the foreseeable future. On the bright side, I might even appear quaintly myopic which would enhance my famously irritating, eccentric behavior. I could wow people with a pair of pinc nez balancing on the tip of my nose.

In a mad moment, I thought Milady Universe may have sent me a heads-up quest – one of *Her* killer interventions containing at least one sinister caveat thrown in for good measure. She and I have had several run-ins of this nature. Milady and her evil twin, Lady Luck, often tossed several penalties into the mix during one of their diversions, otherwise known as dire consequences. Overkill under pressure was their forte.

The truth is, I hadn't been productive of late. As a confirmed worrywart I was deeply conflicted about self-publishing an art history book and anguished over its unforeseen expenditures. Nothing eclipsed my whinging about the unfairness of life, nor halted the progression of my paradoxically indifferent depression, and I was exhausted from counting imagined landmines in my sleep.

So, a test wrapped in a fairy-tale just might be what the doctor ordered to jumpstart a creative lull.

In true Brothers Grimm mode, I sensed a surge of Piscean

energy settle on my life and envisioned myself as a passerby waylaid by an enchanted fish in need of a favor, in exchange for which, it would offer me a reward I couldn't refuse. My first thought was to escape down the nearest rabbit hole. My second was the impossibility of digging to the center of the earth. My third thought was to take the day off and go fishing.

Temptation with a sting in its 'tale' might be Madame Universe's perverse way of wishing me a happy birthday. If so, I reasoned there may be a chance of outwitting an overconfident invincible witchy woman. I was nothing if not cunning. What could possibly go wrong.

Well, for a start, I was completely wrong. After twenty-four hours of false bravado my little fantasy only served to reaffirm my habitual grey sky thinking. A wishy-washy canopy was hardly the miracle sky to set me free. More than ever, I believed everything in life began and ended murkily, and that nothing worth attaining was miniscule.

My failures were legendary climbing missions routinely involving serious mountaineering equipment. I deliberately sabotaged my life at every opportunity and took no prisoners, or so my friends liked to tell me.

To scale the present Mt. Everest of medical challenges I required altitude, smelling salts, and a Sherpa in the form of a Saint Bernard rescue dog bearing an enormous flask of brandy.

I scrutinized my options with a Sherlock Holmes size

magnifying glass. Where was I supposed to go? Could I hide out in plain sight as my invisible friend Leonardo suggested? How was I to cope? Could an astrological hiccup account for everything negative in my life? It appeared as if it did.

It was time to paint a sweet baby-blue canopy with fluffy clouds. Robin's egg would be nice or better yet, aquamarine. Surely aquamarine could mollify a trickster fish, no problem.

In desperation, I begged Milady to send me her best Sherpa.

CHAPTER 2 - **SIGHT UNSEEN**

A fish won't do anything, but swim in a brook
He can't write his name or read a book
To fool the people is his only thought
And though he's slippery, he still gets caught
But then if that sort of life is what you wish
You might grow up to be a fish!

'Swinging on a Star' – Johnny Burke

My name is Stella Avon. I am fifty-two years old. Old being the operative word when you outlive your usefulness to society. My 'best-by expiry date' had been far from certain, but impaired vision bodes ill for maintaining a foothold in the publishing world I had yet to establish with any significant success.

As a self-appointed historian in my chosen field (the Italian Renaissance) my radical theory was pinned to a lucid dream I'd had about Leonardo da Vinci when I was a seventeen-year-old student in my first year of art college.

Michael Grant, a college acquaintance, had hooked me on Leonardo the day we attended a field trip to London's National Gallery. But before Michael became my personal da Vinci tutor and taught me to fly… before the renaissance dream, I was a fish out of water drowning in self pity.

I never wanted to let go of my Leonardo dream. But in time, the *dream* let go of *me*. Until, that is, my last birthday when recurring waking visions returned and Leonardo urged me to write it all down. *"For posterity's sake,"* he said. *"You don't need to fuss. Mirror writing was torture for me, but I used it to prove I was more important than everyone else. I also had an issue with trust. I was nothing if not troubled before we met."*

Leonardo had been more than an hallucination, a spontaneous visitation, or an abstract voice from the past. More companion than friend. He was one of my inner voices aligned to the truth.

It was easy to be blindsided by Leonardo's attention. I am embarrassed to admit I was initially smitten by his celebrity.

The elder Leonardo da Vinci's devotion was no minor conquest. But flattery blinded me to the obvious: he was not yet the grand master of his later years. Like me, he was a scared kid, angry with his parents. A tad insecure, acting out for momentum's sake.

My Leonardo was a young, troubled teenager. We were kindred. He'd been abandoned by a dysfunctional family. We grew up alone, 500 years apart; yet together we were as close as one soul. Our dreams grew bolder. We spoke of intimate things, blinded by harmless puppy love.

Strangely, the closer Leonardo and I became, my love for Michael grew until I had no time for childish fantasies.

Michael courted me after Leonardo fell silent. In a way, he seemed like an extension of Leonardo.

But in the beginning, Leonardo and I spoke often. I whispered hello every evening under the stars.

His answer came pronto. "*Buongiorno mia cara. Ca va?* How goes it?"

"I miss you."

"I must work now. We will meet later tonight, *si*?"

"Yes. I will wait forever."

His nightly presence became a source of comfort. I fell in love with a shy gentle boy. We trusted each other, safe in the knowledge we could never meet. We played out our growing pains on a never-ending 'blind date with innocent benefits'.

I know one's first love is supposed to last forever, and maybe it did. But Leonardo, mapped out for greatness, required solitude, and after a time, Michael and I became inseparable and dreamed new dreams.

Today, in a mad moment, I dared to defy my cold-hearted star, publish immediately, determined to let the historical evidence arrive naturally in good time.

An inexplicable voice in my head, I'd thought long since banished returned to advise me so. "The cheese stands alone," it whispered. "It's time to stand up to a bully with no spine." The message became insistent and more frequent. A curious puzzle. I took the bait.

I'd had mantras before in my 'Findhorn life' as a mystical student. But nothing as strong as this cheesy one. I stifled the death star by mentally plugging my ears and stood alone, feeling rather cold but extraordinarily special.

A lot was riding on a verbal contract with a young literary agent as wet behind the ears as me. And so, I stood alone, traveling under a cosmic curse, slightly shaken with a bombshell prognosis ticking in my pocket. Unsettling days lay ahead.

I chose the sea as a place to process my forced retirement and rethink my plan of defense in a more nurturing environment. And in the unlikely event, should I still choose to resist the inevitable, it was healthier to inhale sea air than traffic fumes for a clear head. I had decisions to make. Naturally, in keeping with my present attitude, I rented an isolated beach house, sight unseen, to make a point. I needed to decompress.

Barking Dog Island rang an uncanny bell considering there was every indication I might soon become 'barking mad'. It was connected to the mainland of Vancouver Island by a causeway that disappeared every evening and became a serviceable road by noon the next day. I took it as a sign that an isolated cottage at the end of a trail of phantom breadcrumbs was the perfect place for a dogmatic woman playing blindman's bluff to dematerialize one pixel at a time. I likened my situation to watching the reverse process of a polaroid image turning into a white square.

My half-baked plan was to take the coward's way out if all else failed. To this sad end, I brought enough sleeping pills to knock out a Clydesdale.

No-one would know I'd gone. No-one would miss me, or my paper theories burned on a beach. My vain pipedream of creating a literary stir in the halls of academia would blow away in a silent hiss of smoke and ashes.

Geographically speaking, I had come to the far end of nowhere. My front door was separated from the water by a narrow strip of white beach and a lopsided swell of dunes like a row of misshapen camels' humps, choked with thatch grass.

Despite my derring-do, in my heart of hearts I remained separated from reality by the fearsome belief I was being watched by a demon star with a reputation to defend.

I moved to my island on an overcast Sunday afternoon in a summer squall that levitated an eerie carpet of fine sand into a low cloud. Its swirling motion reminded me of the theatrical effects of dry ice to simulate an otherworldly setting. Perfect.

I strode through it purposefully on goddess-sized legs, fooling no-one, determined to appear in charge. Wraparound sunglasses hid my eyes, red from crying jags, and protected me from airborne sand but not the paranoia of being judged by a celestial bully waiting to strike.

Foolishly, I thumbed my nose at the gathering storm clouds, and the ghostly sound of a frantic dog barking far away and concluded the best way to resolve a serious challenge was by hiding my head in the sand. I chose to let sleeping dogs lie by ignoring my problem head on, eyes front, pretending to believe an ethereal landscape was a poetic metaphor for a brave new world.

And for 24 hours I *felt* brave. The head-in-the-sand approach did the trick.

As my first order of defiance, I'd driven alone over a dodgy unfamiliar route without a license. In my second, I unpacked several boxes of eye-straining books that a team of doctors told me *not* to read, refrigerated bags of comforting junk food after being ordered to eat salads, and opened one of two hefty boxes of jelly donuts.

My staples of teabags, sugar, cream, and blurry books awaited. Later, I shoved the white cane my doctor gave me under the bed out of sight. "Practise with this even though you might not need it," he'd said. "And if you'd like, I can arrange a therapy animal for you. If worst comes to worst you may need to get used to a trained guide dog in the future but in the meantime, any dog from the SPCA is excellent company. You're far too dour to be alone." He patted the top of my head as if I was a dog. "Keep in touch, my dear. And don't wait too long for the surgery. There's a good girl."

I sprayed lemon zest ahead of me as I toured the charming premises, wielding the can like a machete to detox the stale smell of karmic abandonment only to find the cottage had been cleared of all furniture or indications that anyone had lived there for quite some time. The domain of a spartan. I would need the courage and self-discipline of a spartan to win my war.

The electricity was on but other than functioning kitchen appliances, flickering ceiling lights, and an open box of jelly donuts, the cottage was bare as old Mother Hubbard's cupboard.

On initial assessment, I wandered upstairs and down, through seaside rooms void of dust and fingerprints, without the slightest whiff of former habitation.

But backtracking to the kitchen I saw something I couldn't possibly have missed on the first round. A framed art print leaned against the stairwell, its non-glare glass, cracked and split diagonally with the loose shards removed and presumably disposed of safely as there were no fragments of broken glass to be found nearby.

The exposed print showed a painting so familiar to me that I might have painted it myself had I possessed the talent and lived 500 years ago. I had sketched the thing on an art school outing when I was a teenager.

The honk of the moving van put the mystery on hold. The next hour was a flurry of activity, redirecting furniture to various locations, and holding back the beach that arrived on the soles of movers' work boots. I swept what sand I could from contaminating my spotless rooms that had surprisingly taken possession of me.

A mover approached shamefacedly with the bill. He stood looking very 'cap in hand' without the cap. "I'm very sorry ma'am," he said. "I think we let your dog out by mistake."

As I signed the receipt, distant barking came from the sand dunes. "It will come back, no doubt," I replied. "Dogs will be dogs."

The previous tenant had left me little more than the scent of cleaning products in gentle seashore rooms, but as it turned out, the print was a godsend.

Outside, downwind, I removed what remained of glass shards and let the wind take the crystals of powdered glass so as not to aggravate my eyes or scratch what I recognized as an expensive gallery-quality print of Verrocchio's 15th century painting 'Tobias and the Angel' – an obscure choice but one entirely familiar to me. I thought I knew it inside and out.

In contrast to my pale rooms, the 'Tobias' is a bright narrative painting of primary blues, reds, and yellows that delivers a biblical scene of an open road where a boy, accompanied by his faithful prancing dog, an enchanted fish caught and strung onto a wooden carrying stick, and the angel Raphael, travelling incognito, journey together on a quest of compassionate intervention.

Where had it come from? And when? I was not yet blind in the conventional sense, so I could never have walked past it without recognition, let alone missed it entirely. Some parasitic polyp lodged in my brain was already playing tricks.

But polyps aside, if logic failed me, I had a last-ditch weapon lurking inside a box of old spiritual books packed with accompanying meditation aids: beeswax candles, sandalwood incense, a brass 'singing bowl', a smooth green bloodstone bequeathed to me by Michael, whom I'd promised to marry, and a bamboo wind chime from the ecological Findhorn Community in Scotland where we spent a gap year after art school.

When I was eighteen, spirit had touched me there in serendipitous ways. Findhorn became my compass of choice for measuring how far on or off the path to enlightenment I was. But after one blissful year, an innocent astrology workshop ushered in an unexpected demon, I became starstruck and lost my way.

For many years, my inner voice and I debated the pros and cons of returning to Findhorn in heated waves of truth or dare. But I became proficient at shouting it down until it swept itself under a carpet.

Meanwhile, the relentless surf of Vancouver Island's west coast pounded like a steady heartbeat – my life's blood flowed with intakes and outtakes of the moon's breath.

Hopes of a seaside cure surfaced playfully, and for a while the evening sky felt friendly. My fond memories of universal love, no doubt still twitched in the abandoned floorboards and rafters of Findhorn. They called my name from inside the Findhorn box. *Open Me. Come Home, Stella. All is forgiven.*

CHAPTER 3 – **FINDHORN FEVER**

"To err is human; to forgive is canine."

Findhorn was a joyous phantom long before it manifested on the A96 – as fictional as Rivendell or Narnia and especially, Bilbo's Shire.

The word 'Findhorn' triggered a thunderbolt quickening in my solar plexus almost simultaneously with meeting the *'second first love* of my life'. Michael Grant saved me from the creative blues I'd been forced to endure. If I couldn't be a painter girl then surely, I was fortunate to love and be loved by an ardent painter *boy*.

I'd informed my parents I was an artist as soon as I could hold a paintbrush. *'That's nice dear'* was their response and nothing more was said. The poor things had no idea who they were dealing with. I had limitless powers. But when I turned sixteen, my father read me the riot act regarding extended education. He wouldn't hear of painting as a career.

'Artists lead poverty-stricken lives,' he said. *'But commercial art has validity'*. Moreover, it was where he intended to invest in my future financial independence.

Unwittingly, the choice of an English art school in my parent's hometown gave me Michael.

In the first semester of school, I fell in love three times: first with Leonardo da Vinci, followed closely by the New-Age Community of Findhorn, and most importantly, Michael, the true love of my life who I abandoned in a selfless act of sacrifice.

For months I ignored my curriculum of graphic design and consumed art history books, basking in Michael's shadow, until his tutorials changed my life.

Synchronicity played a significant part. After Michael introduced me to his idol Leonardo da Vinci, a book crossed my path that someone left on his easel entitled 'The Magic Garden of Findhorn'. Destiny called. I was starstruck. I had to go there.

Sometimes, to balance the score, Milady Universe plays the eternal game of 'double-dog dare you' – a game never intended for the half-baked intentions of a woeful child like me.

I talked up the joys of Findhorn for two years until my relentless six-star reviews finally convinced Michael it was as near to Utopia as an earthling may be permitted entrance. *'One day'*, he promised. *'I will take you to Findhorn for our honeymoon if you promise to stop pestering me. I'm sold, okay!'* But fate conspired to advance our visit in ways beyond coincidental.

Michael formally asked for my hand in marriage, and we drove north to the highlands of Scotland so I could meet his parents.

Cora and Drew Grant lived in an isolated cottage in the county of

Ross, on a finger of land nosing into the Moray Firth. I had assumed isolated was another word for bleak, but I was mistaken. Everything glowed with the quickened synergy of a rosy future.

Walking the chilly cliffs and beaches was invigorating, and then, one morning over tea and scones, Michael blindsided me with an unexpected announcement.

It must be stated that Michael Grant revealed hidden truths better than anyone I've ever known. His eyes danced when he was privy to a mysterious secret. On the morning in question, his face was flushed, and he ignored his favorite breakfast of Cora's currant scones and bitter Scottish marmalade. Worse, a stickler for hot tea, he'd allowed his tea to grow cold. Michael's energy was off the scale. He was overexcited. I'd never seen him so stirred up.

When I felt his forehead, he seized my hand and kissed it.

"I'm not ill. I'm over the moon," he said. "I'm bursting with a belated 'welcome to Scotland' surprise, for *you*. But you'll have to wait. I can't show you until it's dark. A night sky is required."

I was caught by his enthusiasm. "What could possibly top a night under the stars with you?"

Michael covered the palm of my hand with fervent kisses and held it to his cheek. I felt his grin widen. "My surprise will blow your beautiful little mind," he said.

"Is it a telescope? Are we going star gazing?"

He winked. His eyes twinkled. "Sort of, but more magical.

And by more, I mean cosmic. Think astronomical magic."

"Goodness, you're scaring me. As magic as that!"

Michael held my face and stared into my eyes. "I love you completely, Stella. I would give you the sun, the moon, and the stars if it were in my power."

My gift unfolded that night from atop a rocky outcrop overlooking the Moray Firth. Michael stood behind me, resting his chin on my shoulder. He kissed my neck and pointed to a group of moving lights flying in formation like a squadron of UFO's. "Let our halcyon days commence," he said, squeezing my arm.

"Wow unidentified flying… *um*… saucers? That's not something you see everyday."

Michael twisted me to face him. "I'm afraid not, sweet pea. I'm pleased to identify them as a squadron of planes from…" he paused… "Kinloss Airforce Base!"

He waited in silence while his words sank in. I smiled innocently until a memory quickened. I gasped. "Did you say Kinloss!"

Michael casually raised an eyebrow. "I believe I did."

Kinloss, a place synonymous with Findhorn, had bequeathed the community its Main Street - an abandoned wartime landing strip. Organic buildings had sprouted its length like the banks of an enchanted river. And there it floated, minutes away as the crow flies and several picturesque hours driving around lochs and herds of highland sheep.

Michael explained he'd only half-listened to my Findhorn praises, never placing it near his old home until his mother asked him if he'd received the Findhorn book that she'd sent to the college via Phillip Moon, one of her old school chums who, as it happened, taught my favorite drawing class.

Before being presented in a visual format, Findhorn had been an empty sound byte Michael blocked out as his mother's nonstop spiritual mumbo jumbo. Now halcyon was the operative word for a blissful marriage.

We drove to Findhorn primed to enter nothing less than middle-earth and crossed the threshold from our old life into an eco-community of palpably conscious love.

Findhorn *was* the Shire!

We strolled the main loop from the car park to the Universal Hall, two giddy humans in love – a single spiral of human light levitating under a magic spell.

When we returned to our car, someone had left a small card under a wiper blade that read: *my karma ran over my dogma.* We were home, infected with the uncontrollable joy of giggling.

The first of many workshops I attended in Findhorn blindsided me with aromatherapy. I entered a room, parted a welcoming curtain of scent with my body, and entered the sacred space behind it where a few drops of lemongrass essential oil simmered in water, infusing the room with peace. I remember the moment now as an essential awakening.

It was a defining moment of calm that stayed. I took to carrying a miniature bottle of 'cymbopogan citratus' with me as an emergency restorative, used sparingly as organic smelling salts. Whenever I inhaled it, I was transported to Findhorn. Lemongrass was 'time-travel' in a bottle. The remains of my original bottle were buried in the Findhorn Box. Perhaps a ghost of its power remained.

Lesser-known Findhorn hypnotics were equally powerful: the breathtaking sight of low flying swans in a Scottish mist, Earl Grey tea infused with bergamot, Dundee cake on a rainy afternoon, and the community's midnight parade of glowing handmade lanterns made of rice paper, accompanied by Gregorian chant – a Findhorn tradition bringing in the winter solstice.

That said, and as irrational as it may be, I still blame Findhorn for inspiring the destructive romance with astrology that unleashed my present troubles because I inadvertently called down a life of suffering when I hired a budding astrologer to cast my chart.

Michael was not in favor. He shook his head and murmured "very dodgy," whenever he saw me absorbed in an astrology book. Later, when I became obsessed, he grabbed the book away from me with a melodramatic warning. "You're opening a can of pseudo-scientific worms with this drivel," he said. "Just so you know. If it gets out of hand, things could get messy for us."

I proceeded against his advice, feeling sorry for Tari, a harmless girl with a self-appointed affinity for reading stars, who openly swooned over Michael.

According to Tari's reading, Sirius, the dog star, had appeared as a misty presentation on July 3, 1970, the day of my birth. Had the star shone clear in the heavens, my story would have been vastly improved. Tari declared me a hapless victim of predestined circumstance and predicted enough gloom and tragedy to sink my soul. And if that hadn't clinched a canine curse, I was informed I had also been born under a 'void of course' moon. There was no misinterpreting that level of doom.

Michael tried to set me straight. But for once, his spiritual wisdom seemed trite and unkind. "So," he admonished, "You're going to believe Pollyanna's dimwitted evil twin?"

I countered innocently with "You believe in synchronicity so surely we must investigate whatever comes our way."

Michael's disappointment frightened me. "Astrology is an illogical slippery slope of unicorn rubbish," he argued. "You can't possibly believe stars are sentient or that they affect the fate of humans. For what? Cosmic amusement? Do you really believe humans progress through the houses of the zodiac for some grandiose purpose?"

"But what if we do? Isn't the truth supposed to set us free."

Michael sighed, brushed the hair from my eyes, and kissed the tip of my nose. "It should but it hardly ever does. For some reason humans are hell bent on suffering. Keats' epitaph is a case in point: *'Here lies one whose name is writ in water.'* "Not a confident happy guy, in the end."

I stubbornly refused to yield to commonsense. Saving face became more important than being right.

With the most loving of intentions, Michael felt obliged to give me some space. I felt abandoned and fumed even more. Our failure to agree to disagree terminated in a painful death under the stars.

Michael's eyes held mine as he rubbed my shoulders. "Come back to me, Stella. This isn't who we are," he said.

A nastiness descended upon me. I squirmed out of his arms and pushed him away. My words were meant to wound. I spat venom to make a final point. "Maybe Tari was right. According to our sun signs, she says we are in astrological opposition. Maybe we're not meant to be together."

After that spiteful declaration I withdrew into a permanent sulk. We reluctantly agreed on a temporary separation, during which my mission to save Michael escalated to an obsessive need to prove my worthiness and so, a month later, in the bleakest of midwinters, Michael left the dogma/karma card propped on the mantelpiece with a white rose. He wrote *'till death parts us'* on the back.

Eventually, he left the country without a forwarding address, and I deserted Findhorn like a thief in the night.

Tari gave me a 'cup of destiny' as a whimsical parting gift - an ironic fortune telling device that reduced the murky 'science' of divination to a parlor game.

So much for astronomical calculations. Michael and I were a pair of star-crossed victims - a footnote in Tari's diary… a couple of horoscopes that passed in the night.

Michael was right, of course. He always did the math. He knew that the fortunes of men, while serendipitous, could never be influenced by the haphazard position of stars or sentient tealeaves.

But I had nurtured a deep-seated irrational fear of being happy since childhood. English parents during the generation of being 'seen and not heard' made me unworthy of opinions. And so, when I was pretending to be a princess marked out for greatness, a dogged bug of superstition laid eggs in my brain, and I wasn't about to take chances. Michael didn't deserve to suffer. I did.

Fixed laws aligned to human birth made a mockery of Tari's calculating cruelty of complex mathematics. In turn, my inexcusable lack of insight, a stunning absence of hindsight, and a false sense of heroic pride made a mockery of our vow to never leave each other.

I realized too late; I'd had power all along. So much so, that my unforgivable failure to honor my commitment to my beloved had overruled a love match destined to be.

I mourned Michael as if he'd died but it was *me* who had departed life. And in the madness that followed, it was easier to surrender to the darker laws of prophecy that took the form of a slavering rabid dog.

I had a strong desire to dash the cup against a tree - to smash its unintelligible map of the constellations and scatter its astrological symbols back to a freakish dimension ruled by a false prophet... a slum landlord psychopath named Zodiac.

Naturally, my intention of destroying the cup of destiny, failed. The cup remained gallingly intact after I tossed it into the Findhorn River. It floated out of sight - a carefree blue bowl, lazily spinning in an eddy, dreaming its way to heaven.

I headed for the airport with a haunting vision of a cup of poison caught in a supernatural vortex for eternity. Instinctively, my body shut down in a desperate bid for survival and I flew over the Atlantic in a fever dream, a lost Findhorn girl searching for Michael.

I returned soul damaged to my parents' house where they managed to celebrate my homecoming as an achievement. But the ghosts of Findhorn shadowed me. *'Trust your lucky stars,'* they whispered. *'Come home. Self-fulfilling prophecies are far more dangerous than dragons. Surrender.'*

Keats' sad declaration continued to haunt me. I tried to shake it off, but Shakespeare's *'All the world's a stage, and all the men and women merely players'* confirmed my fears.

Nothing was more depressing than life ruled by a cruel universe and an endless succession of accursed exits and entrances in a meaningless play. If human love was sparked by random chemicals that grew powerless with time, then it was better to have loved and lost. I pretended to be relieved, but I didn't fool anyone, least of all, me.

It was a mercy I slept for days at a time. But whenever I regained consciousness, I allowed Sirius to pull me back into a whirlpool of shame.

I eventually surrendered to proper 'underworld sleep' and woke, broken, in a hospice after months had passed. I felt nothing. Medication kept me semiconscious, and doctors monitored my mental recovery until I was pronounced lucid enough to see a psychiatrist.

Yet, I believed more than ever it had been my sacred mission to free Michael from a malefic force inbred in me. A cold eavesdropping star toying with creation had presented me with an ultimatum that callously drove Michael and I apart without extinguishing Michael's love of art. Word came from Cora that he was painting in Italy.

During this transition, whenever I came close to remembering joy, Keats reminded me I was insubstantial. I felt bloodless. Emptiness rendered me incapable of giving or receiving love. I was invisible - an unworthy poet whose life story would continue to be writ in water.

And then, ironically, I was given art supplies as therapy. *'Paint your way back to life'* a voice said.

CHAPTER 4 - **PAINTING 101**

I ignored the art therapist's suggestion to dabble with fingerpaint and embarked on a series of self-portraits while she sat silently, a little apart from me for support.

Without hesitation, I chose a stick of charcoal and toyed with it in clammy hands. I studied my eyes in a makeup mirror until the rest of my features disappeared. A lost soul stared back at me. "There you are," I said.

"What's left of you," a voice replied.

The therapist shifted in her chair. I sensed her writing notes.

I squinted at the stranger's face and timidly spoke aloud. "Are you my soul?"

The voice corrected me immediately. "Contrary to popular belief, the soul doesn't reside in the eyes. It floats above your head… if you're lucky."

I shifted my gaze. Sure enough, I had what passed for a halo of light an inch above my hair.

I drew that first, then the oval contours of my face without eyes nose or mouth. It was enough. It had taken the better part of the day to accomplish. I blurred the lines with my index finger and smudged in a suggestion of cheekbones. A dark portrait of a human raincloud remained on the paper.

"Aren't you going to sign it?" the therapist asked.

I scrawled my initials S A and crossed them out. "I'm not quite there, yet. Maybe tomorrow."

After several tomorrows, portraits emerged, all without eyes. Then ones with eyes only. And when I'd had enough of eyes, I explored my other senses, adding a nose, ears, and lastly a smear of charcoal where my mouth should be.

Finally, I drew myself in the three-quarter pose of the Mona Lisa, arms folded, a hint of life emerging in the ghost of a rosy smile - an underpainting of sepia wash.

After that, the colors came. I was Vincent's profile with a turquoise and green complexion, wearing a yellow straw hat; Munch's 'Scream' set against an undulating sunset; and the real me - a pained carnival mask with knitted brows, complexion a deathly blue pallor with purple bruises under the eyes. But the day came when I painted a calm woman with an aura of blue sparks emanating from my head like a crown. I started to breathe in irregular spasms.

"Here I am," the stranger said. "Welcome home."

I found the faculty to crack a joke. "I must be lucky, then."

"I never specified," the voice came back. "Think positive. After all, bad luck is still luck!"

Leonardo surprised me on the eve of my twenty-first birthday. I was near sleep when he whispered *"Happy birthday, my angel. Cara, don't you know by now that I forgave you a long time ago. All that stands between you and love is forgiving yourself. I have always seen you through the eyes of love. A domani di ieri… more than yesterday less than tomorrow."*

His words were food of the gods but being unworthy of such devotion, I swallowed a couple of sleeping pills and hid from his love under headphones thumping with rock music.

Leonardo had painted me a loving vision of the future, but I continued to numb my memories of Michael and Findhorn with fake willpower and depression medication. My victim mindset believed the ill-fated thread of life, mapped out for me in the Dog Star's labyrinth of rebirth.

I had suffered a massive spiritual heart attack and faced a new world based on an old self-fulfilling prophecy with nothing remotely akin to courage - a pale romantic figure, martyrdom accomplished. I was dog tired.

I viewed suffering as scoring brownie points with Mother Universe, and so, I welcomed my days as a bereft painter reduced to designing advertising campaigns in commercial print shops. And although they were visual artforms, they were never about easels and oil paint or the glorious scent of linseed oil.

Thankfully, I was spared further visual reminders of Michael painting in his Italian studio.

Guilt, remorse, and regret continued to haunt me until 2000, when a rare flash of millennium energy afforded me four years of respite. Sirius grew too faint to wield power over me and I enrolled in a university course to earn a belated Fine Arts degree. For once, paint was mine and art history was more than a hobby.

But perhaps because of my insolence, depression dogged me anew. I wore a badge of shame for having the audacity to call myself an artist.

Leonardo's timely intervention to document my experiences failed to offset the years I'd wasted. Writing was Leonardo's form of catharsis; not mine. And although I once dabbled in poetry inspired by love's young dream, my heart was never in dredging up a memoir of accumulated blunders.

In 1988 I'd thought nothing could sabotage my happiness, but it did. I was 18 when I met Findhorn and 19 when I said goodbye.

It was still 'The Shire' the day I left. Milady Universe's mantle of wanton stars sent me a continuous stream of dragons.

Sometimes, synchronicity takes half a lifetime to wave a white flag. But being riddled with guilt, it took a major cosmic intervention, a wishing fish, and man's best friend for me to feel worthy of forgiveness.

It turned out Sirius's bite was far worse than its bark.

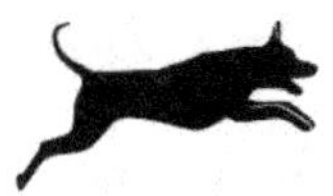

CHAPTER 5 - **TOBIAS and the ANGEL**

'Swinging on a Star' – Johnny Burke

Twenty-five hours after my arrival on Barking Dog Island I sat before the painting, listening for its secret. A message arrived in no uncertain terms: *"Look inside the Findhorn box. It's time to look inside yourself. You are not alone. Help is there. Look. Listen. Find it."*

When an abandoned box of memorabilia calls it's always an omen with a double-edged invitation to face unfinished business. The lid took some effort to open and unstuck suddenly with somewhat of a melodramatic pop. I stopped breathing.

The scent of lemongrass and the disturbed ghost of an engagement ring, long since lost, floated out, screaming past me.

The gauntlet was down. It was up to me to stay or follow a nervous thread into an age-old labyrinth I'd only vaguely acknowledged that I'd come to find by the sea. According to my doctor, without surgery I may only have a few months before surrender would no longer be a timely option.

I hadn't entirely known what I was searching for until a hard object slid with a clunk from under a wad of paper clippings,

It was a parting talisman from Michael – a smooth worry stone kept under my pillow at night and carried against the terrible transition years during lapses of mind-numbing loneliness and regret.

The cold weight of it in my hand quickened and unleashed a guarded memory of my darling lost boy, quite possibly, dead.

I heard myself laughing in sobs. The floor met me halfway, its hardwood bruising my knees. My thumb found the well-worn depression on one side of the stone. Warm electricity flooded my hand. I felt the urge to runaway to sea and I realized with a wry shock that I had. I felt a strong urge to prevent a circle from closing. At least one that would leave me on the outside. I felt an irrational need to hold open a door that wasn't there.

"You're in shock," an inner voice chastised. "Be careful. Please. There be dragons. Haven't you had enough!"

"I intend to," I replied. "Angels fear to tread and all that bosh."

I needed a cup of sweet tea and fast. It was how Londoners coped during the blitz. Tea was the first line of defence against trauma. The British knew the power of sugar during rough times. "And if I'm in for the war I think I am," I griped to the voice. "I need to perk up. My soul is in tatters."

The voice continued. "But the doctor…" it changed its tack. "Stella, it's too soon. Please put down that dreadful box. Your timing is off. I urge you to wait. Timing is everything."

I closed my eyes and hugged the box. "This box is not full of dread. It may yet save me. Hang the consequences. I'm already a victim of an *old* war. Assuredly, this *new* one won't be a fair fight. Now, be an angel and go away." The voice chuckled.

I made the tea strong enough to melt a spoon and inhumanly sweet and rummaged inside the box.

The dog-eared pages of Alan Watts' philosophical books lay atop a manilla file emblazoned with the words: astrology chart for Stella Avon in bold red letters. Angry bees stung the inside of my stomach. I tore the chart in half and then in a temper tantrum, shredded it into confetti.

I grabbed one of Alan Watts' books, opened it to a random page, and read one of his celestial witticisms describing the cosmos as *'a fireworks display of radioactive mud and gas'*. His words formed a speech bubble that hovered over my head. It contained a message too on-the-nose to hear: *'Just LISTEN dear heart. The truth will set you free. Write your life in peacock blue ink.'*

I swept up the torn paper and tossed it into the fire where it exploded in a ghastly smell of stale hope. Alan was nothing if not profound. I didn't deserve his help. I was not through suffering.

I convinced myself that missing paintings showed up all the time – the purview of some universal lost & found operating under grace and favour. Attics, basements, garage sales, and junk shops revealed treasures every day. A stairwell may be less undercover, but it was just as effective.

My 'Tobias' was only a print – technically, a ghost of the original. It had obviously been hiding-in plain-sight at the farthest edge of my peripheral vision, and in my eagerness to feel above the laws of physics, I had been momentarily disoriented by the barking dog.

Leonardo da Vinci's rising star was born to rave reviews, April 15, 1452, with Sirius, no doubt, burning brightly beyond a brilliant cerulean-blue Tuscan sky.

In 1467, at the age of fifteen, Leonardo had already been a lowly apprentice in the bustling workshop of Andrea del Verrocchio for two years. Like all students, Leonardo's introduction to the business of art began with a few basic drawing exercises but mostly by shadowing senior apprentices while performing the never-ending tasks of a studio dogsbody.

Leonardo displayed his natural abilities as a draftsman, early, but when he was seventeen, he rose overnight from the ranks of mediocrity as a wunderkind due to a contract for a large narrative painting depicting the biblical parable of 'Tobias and the Angel'.

Verrocchio immediately designated it a 'studio painting' – a team effort to be executed by senior artists and apprentices alike who were assigned specific sections according to their experience. The least promising students shared the extraneous background details: a lowly clump of grass, a cloud, or a rock. Luckily, their bungles were overshadowed by the elaborate robes of a wealthy angel painted by Sandro Botticelli, no less.

But Leonardo had displayed enough promise to be singled out to illustrate two key elements: an excitable dog and an enchanted fish. His instinctive naturalistic style was so innovative, legend has it, Master Verrocchio hailed Leonardo as a child genius and never painted again. A fabrication with a hint of truth.

By the time Leonardo, died on May 2, 1519, he'd reigned supreme as a scientist, engineer, mathematician, inventor, anatomist, painter, sculptor, architect, botanist, musician, poet, and writer – the definitive sixty-seven-year-old perpetual renaissance man-child.

But sadly, as in life, so it is with paint: oil and water fail to mix. And so, Leonardo's little dog, executed in the new untried medium of oils, failed to adhere to a laid background of egg tempura.

Leonardo's charming terrier showed signs of transparency almost immediately, deteriorating much the same way his 'Last Supper' fresco, thirty years later, crumbled after it failed to sufficiently fuse to an untried recipe for plaster.

Even under strictly regulated conservation controls, the dog's time is running out.

Leonardo was a star-crossed artist. He rarely finished a work and to his detriment, experimented with questionable materials. His commissions, beset with troublesome consequences tended to lose money: 'The Battle of Anghiari' masterpiece with its tortured composition of terrified horses, was entirely painted over by a lesser artist a hundred years after his death; the portrait of 'Ginevra Benci' lost a third of its height and part of its width from an unknown hand; the sitter for 'The Mona Lisa' remained a controversial subject, and Leonardo's lax attention to chemistry resulted in a 'dog's breakfast' of a disastrous 'Last Supper'.

I had planned to edit the Leonardo chapter of my book, first, so the phantom print of the 'Tobias' materializing as it had was both significant and sad. My old belief in synchronicity quickened but bad timing reinforced the injustices of star-spangled disappointments I knew so well.

A few magical years in the spiritual retreat of Findhorn had given me a taste for meaningful coincidences. But those were the days prior to my catastrophic introduction to astrology. Planetarily speaking, I was in opposition to myself. One doesn't get less powerful than that.

I wanted to kick something hard enough to injure my foot. If the painting's glass hadn't been broken, I would have smashed it with a hammer.

The voice in my head snickered. "For the love of dog. You *did* break it. Remember? You said you were going to fight. So, when are you going to take a stand? When!"

I was taken aback. "What? Against the universe?"

"Yes."

"I may have been a tad premature."

"T'would give Star Wars a whole new meaning."

"No thanks. I'm already a casualty of such a war."

"Suit yourself. You always do," the voice said smugly. "But remember, a star can die. Martyrs can outlive their sacrifices."

I was an impressionable teenager. I had wanted to believe in transcendental love and light and was easily swayed but a nagging doubt nibbled away the dream of being partnered with an interactive universe. Equality with the source of omnipotent power was a step beyond my self-worth.

Wanting to believe and believing are entirely different kettles of fish. Wanting is never enough, and so my thoughts settled into a cold pall of abandonment. And as for the occasional flirtation with wishful thinking, there was no loveliness in it. Misery always squares happiness. And so, I excused my clash with New-Age sensitivities as a self-indulgent experiment with the supernatural.

I ran with infamy, the closest thing I had to fame, and to

confirm the celestial diagnosis, I created a fanciful birth certificate – a mental 'horror-scope' riddled with omens and predictions of 'failure to thrive'. I came to believe my own press and accepted the grand title of 'unworthy to succeed'. It's been a slippery slope to depression and anxiety ever since.

In any case, it was impossible to accept I might be a potential superstar living on a benevolent megastar. Besides, the poetic notion that humanity was fashioned from stardust, rankled. It was too picture-perfect for me.

Ashamed of dabbling in make-believe, I'd hitched my embarrassment to an ill-fated star with a reputation for painful side-effects. How could I have done otherwise? The dog star twinkled and winked slyly at me, daring me to resist. I caved under its influence, a tormented guilt-ridden victim and lost my appetite for joy. I consoled myself that I'd saved Michael, rarely reflecting on what we had lost.

Since 1987, the constellation Canis Major, the greater dog, has shaken me in its rabid jaws, but at least it gave me a unique identity, and more importantly, an excuse for failure.

I'd kept my spiritual books and tapes from those idealistic Findhorn days, as an homage to Michael. As much as I sacrificed our future, I couldn't bring myself to destroy four years of loving memories. I remember my mood and the hour I put them away. I stored them carefully, sadly, lovingly with Michael's presence, my teenage diaries, and the sacred objects of meditation practice reduced to powerless souvenirs.

Dancing under a witchy moon was a feminine fantasy; chanting and humming mantras seemed like a wasteful pursuit of time.

In effect, I stepped back, examined the bigger picture of making a living, and opted for what is euphemistically called growing up. But growing up meant giving up, and as a precociously dogged child, my way of giving up included holding on to a mystical toybox of conscious treats. Michael always said I was a mystery of mixed intentions.

I yielded to the dire predictions of the dog star, in mourning, bitter, comatose, and abandoned by thunderbolt love, joined a dreary unemployment line, and accepted a mechanical destiny of banal employment on an unconscious learning curve headed for a career in commercial art that I didn't want.

Whenever I grew wistful for oil paint, in my 'second life' as a self-abandoned martyr, I gave my head a shake.

The extraordinary was a dream too far. And before I knew it, I was a jaded property owner suffocated by debt, fretting under a prophecy of catastrophic failure.

My current visions are best defined as limited. Mother Universe chose wisely to remove them altogether so that all that was left to 'see' was internal turbulence.

I envision myself as a shard of broken glass, agitating in a slurry of seawater and sand for thirty-three years, hoping to be tamed into a gem of polished sea glass. Maybe in my next life.

And yet, something had made me load the Findhorn box in my car at the last moment which meant it was the first box to enter my new home. That had to mean something. I put it down to a nagging muscle memory of a glorious love affair – supressed guilt hounding me for old time's sake.

I fished out Michael's 'sedative stone' for comfort. It had a natural dip on one side like the bowl of a spoon that my right thumb discovered, released an endorphin – an anxiety inhibitor with a similar effect to a baby's soother. It induced the silence that rises above thought and so I dubbed it my listening stone.

If Universe Mom was throwing a surprise birthday party for me, could enlightenment be far behind. Being aligned to a more forgiving star would be worth the inconvenience of seeing life through coke bottle lenses for a while. Surely, I had earned a reprieve. Mom was being sly. I allowed myself to believe I was realigned – that the painting was a sign of grace. Had I been forgiven? Was I vindicated? What Shakespeare dreams may manifest?

In the spirit of housewarming, I hung the print as it came, without glass, in the optimum spot across from my bed where it greeted me each day, according to my erratic mood swings.

CHAPTER 6 - **BED UNREST**

'The Love Song of J. Alfred Prufrock' – T.S. Eliot

The phenomena began when darkness fell. Something fishy was going on.

The faint tapping of a bird's beak on the bedroom window at midnight disturbed my sleep. I squinted from my warm bed too settled to shoo it away.

After it persisted several days, I gave up and accepted a nocturnal bird had been programmed to serenade and unsettle my personal haven. But once I'd given up hearing it as an enemy, the tapping evolved into a pleasant lullaby. I pretended it was the gentle ticking of a clock, gave my thoughts over to time passing, and drifted into stillness.

It was only after a week I discovered no such feathered creature existed on the other side of the window.

I panicked. For a terrifying moment, I thought I was being haunted by the future – a white cane sniffing a city sidewalk or a deathwatch beetle inspecting a bleak trail with its feelers tapping a message in Morse code that heralded the death knell of carefree strolling.

The sounds persisted. Sometimes in the kitchen or on the

stairs, but louder in the evenings, shadowing the measured steps I took up the stairs before diving into the well of unconsciousness known as dreaming one's life away.

Out of sight out of mind wasn't working. The elusive art of slumbering soundly escaped me regardless of warm milk, sleeping pills, and audio tapes of white noise and thunderstorms.

Insomnia, my unwelcome companion, laid eggs in my brain.

The beaks returned as a renewed staccato of fear. I tossed listlessly until my legs were strangled by sheets. My bedroom felt like a haunted elevator stuck in the basement of pre-sleep where restless memories played out on strips of melting celluloid. The future looped by in a nightmarish parade of aliens performing eye surgeries with long creepy fingers.

I called to the voices for help.

A determined voice responded instantly as if it had been waiting close by. *"Remember your deep breathing exercises,"* it said. *"Meditate. Listen to your stone. Rise above thought. Heed what comes."*

I isolated a pattern of claws skittering over the kitchen linoleum. "Oh my god. Do I have rats?"

The voice chuckled. *"That's one thing you'll never have to worry about,"* it said.

I was peeved. "So glad to have amused you."

"Ditto. Higher frequency conversations are a refreshing break from suffering and strife. I have to say, you're hard work."

At that, my dreamy friend must have departed via the open window. Its exit issued in the subtle scents of new-mown grass and earth after the rain that wafted over me like the song of a sacred timepiece. I slept, blissful as a wanted child.

As for the 'dying of the light, from which one is urged to rage against', I received regular pep talks from my doctors. *'It's mind over matter,'* they said. *'Be tough. Go extra gentle into the night'* one of them advised, *'Dylan Thomas was a gloomy cuss. It's less hassle if one accepts and adapts. Raging against anything is not recommended.'*

"I'll alert the art galleries and let my paintbrushes know," I replied huffily. "Fading and dying are different sides of the same coin. One is inevitable the other is an invitation."

I received a team of raised eyebrows for my analysis.

By my reckoning, heightened senses will soon be all that's left to determine if I have a runny nose. And there is some comfort, I suppose, never knowing if one has egg yolk on their shirt. But with my gazelle days far behind me, would I become a formidable old scold, bumping into things?

I drifted into a crazy mind movie – feeling trapped in a subterranean cave, literally in the dark. The tapping was water dripping from a ceiling of stalagmites.

A familiar voice shouted from the mouth of the cave. *"Open your eyes girl! Remember what you know."*

"I'm too tired to play games," I whined. "I just want to sleep.

Who the hell are you?"

"You called ME," it answered. *"Who do you think I am?"*

I warmed to the game. "I expect I'm deteriorating into my second childhood. Are you the imaginary childhood friend I never had?"

"I'm a friend you dreamed once."

"It feels as if I'm saving myself."

"Well, it's about time. Congratulations."

And then I remembered a line from Alan Watts and shouted it aloud. "Unstable fireworks of radioactive mud and gas have explosive problems." I replied.

"What else," the voice shouted back.

A bright thought came to me. "A STAR CAN DIE!"

I woke in a sweat knowing what the tapping was. If I was right, diminished eyesight was the least of my problems.

CHAPTER 7 - MATERNAL DYSFUNTION

It was apparent to me that Mother Universe, as perverse as only *She* can be when pregnant with possibilities, had compensated my fixation as a victim of lack with an ironic abundance of migraines. And yet it was strangely comforting to realize she'd also been the all-powerful midwife the morning I was born under a 'bad star'. But how dreadfully minimal, I thought, to fizzle out in such a universally small bang. Pffft!

"Silly girl," the voice said. *"I thought you said the universe was maternal. Wasn't that your wish?"*

I crossed my arms and sighed. "She is when She *wants* to be."

There was a long pause. My inner voice was thinking. *"You do know what they call a female dog, right? For dog's sake thwart the woman! She's not a saint. If you know what's good for you, you'll cut your adopted 'mother's apron strings. Yesterday would have been a fine time; timing is everything."*

"The art of thwarting is overrated," I grumped.

My voice had the last word. *"You mean grovelling is easier."*

Cosmic intelligence answered my call. I braced myself to be frazzled by hindsight rather than dazzled with insight so late in life. One thing remained true and certain: the prospect of being blinded by magic never entered my mind.

But that night, as I prepared for bed, the magic appeared.

"Clearly, the Great Goddess Yin is no pushover," I declared out loud to my face in the dressing table mirror. It nodded. "The Universe is one crazy lady," I added as I applied night cream.

I brushed my hair vigorously. "DNA has a lot to answer for.

My reflection shook its head. "Ah, now I *see*," it replied with contempt. "You're *planning* to fail."

How well it knew me. "Now, you see here," I snapped back, and burst into childish tears.

A plaintive canine whine issued from beneath my chair. A soft apparition jumped into my lap and tried to lick them away. Its compassionate presence broke a damn and I had the best cry of my life.

My Sherpa turned out to be more of a lap dog... one it was impossible to see even while I still could, because it was conjured by my overactive imagination.

CHAPTER 8 - **AMAZING FACE**

"I once was lost but now I'm found.
Was blind but now I see."

Amazing Grace – John Newton

My wakeup call was a revelation. A Goldilocks' critical mass of questionable grace. The future was too small; living large between sunshine and rain felt 'just right'. Extremes blurred into sensations: never too hot never too cold… but never quite right.

I returned to my looking glass often. It was there the world made sense or rather it's where the crazy resided. I could handle crazy. I knew crazy. I was intimately familiar with voices arguing in my head, but I missed the greater voice that once filled me with love. Yet the craziest thing of all was that my reflection had become as wise as the oracle of Delphi.

I've come to know the art of perspective intimately. My shape may be blurred but my mind is sharp. I am strangely unveiled without feeling vulnerable. My night terrors have subsided, tragedy contains an emerging edge of comic relief, and apart from bumping into things, I relish wandering in a muted Turner seascape. The man knew the delights of aquamarine-blue like no other.

I scored my movie with weather and birdsong, and always, the background static of a barking dog persisted. She was as female as the universal goddess who regularly blinded with love, but she would venture no closer. And so, I spent endless days calling *'here girl'* to the dog from another world before realizing *she* was calling *me!*

When it rained, I listened to individual raindrops. When it was fine, I sat by the ocean and counted the beats of silence after each crashing wave. For an interesting exercise, I welcomed the sting of blowing sand in my face. It tasted as salty as I imagined. Strangely, the stench of seaweed and rotting crabs pleasantly grounded me to the beach. Daily nothings made everything precious.

I believed I was preparing myself for the event known as satori… enlightenment. I had returned full circle to the gates of Findhorn and its red stop signs with white lettering that commanded one and all to: STOP worrying!

After a shower, Leonardo's beloved 'sfumato' filled my bathroom confessional. His technique of painting atmospheric mist set me inside a future landscape, where, like his iconic distant mountains, I was out of focus. The colours of me were as soft as the little dog that followed me up and down the stairs and to the beach. Somehow, I found comfort in being a ghost *before* I died. I wondered if anyone else would see me when I was blind. Which begged the question would I even know if I'd died.

I reached out and wrote my name on the glass with a fingertip: STELLA WAS HERE! and whispered, "I am *still* here. I am quite still. Stillness is here. I am the stillness."

My face was an impressionist's portrait. Not a hard edge in sight. I squinted and reappeared in a startlingly sharp closeup. "Ah, there you are," I said.

Fur brushed my ankles. Something cold pressed into my leg and scuttled away on the bathroom tiles. I looked down slightly alarmed. Nothing was there. When I returned to my face it had melted behind a veil of condensation. I looked like a stroke victim. My portrait was a smear of wet paint – a dream of another me in a funhouse mirror. And then I wasn't there at all, and the mirror became a blank square of polished silver. A frame framing nothing. "And there you go again," I said.

And that's how it went for a time. The lost and found of me. From clarity to shadowy images of a horizon-colored ghost. From *'there you are'* to *'here we go again'*. It was useless to argue with what was.

I'd been foolish enough to think that mute acceptance made me stoic. It was laughable to think that playing at surrender would make me a hero. Was I going gentle into blindness? Maybe that was the only way to go anywhere. I tried to conjure the color of blue behind my eyes that I desired for my heavenly sanctuary. Nothing appeared although I knew the spectrum of blue, well.

"Mirrors are silvered glass... a fancy word for grey," the

voice said.

An endless day stretched into evening that dreadful way time has when solitude morphs into wretched loneliness. I stood at the bathroom sink, self abandoned, mind elsewhere, going through the motions of washing my face.

I gave myself a beauty massage with scented soap lathered into white foam, rinsed with splashes of ice-cold water immediately followed by a steaming hot facecloth. I patted my skin dry with a warm towel and peeked hesitantly over it, surveying the empty room.

And then my little companion scratched at the door and materialized as a golden shape. "Ah, there you are," I said.

CHAPTER 9 - **VESPERS**

Vespers – A.A. Milne

I had been lost in self-pity even before my diagnosis and had little connection with the world outside my primary focus of anguish, which is why it took a few days to realize the 'Tobias' was playing a game with me.

Some days, Leonardo's little dog was there, trotting down the road in all its faded glory. Other days it was gone entirely. The troubling fact, and by troubling, I mean curious, was that the rest of the elements in the painting remained intact which meant I was selectively blind. What was even more extraordinary, was that the 'gone dog' had become an audible companion. I had lost sight of or misplaced a *painted* dog.

As implausible as that *sounds*, and in my defense, a sluggish brain can also be of sound mind; 'penny drop' messages carry a distinct eureka payload.

Nevertheless, the ghost dog came and went... or rather, it stayed and disappeared. Had it wandered off to chase a painted rabbit? Was I driving it mad or was it driving me insane? I seem to have misplaced myself.

Losing one's sight is a bitter blow for an artist. But prognosis aside, it's a straightforward concept. In time, some internal dimmer switch will slowly turn up the dark and the world will slink away with me inside it.

After making a call to my doctor, I spilled my magic beans. I expected an argument, but he was cool. He called my fanciful dog a 'project' and was impressed that I'd had the insight to creatively compensate for grieving over an imminent loss. He congratulated me for *'seeing'* (the man *actually* used the word), a way through an otherwise impossible situation. "Write it all down," he said. "If nothing else, it's a wonderful exercise to take your mind off 'seeing' (again his insensitivity knew no bounds).

For now, my blind spots are nonphysical. My life, once painted in broad strokes of primary emotions, are now pale shapes outlined in water-colours with a fine sable brush.

Neither far-sighted nor near-sighted, I still speak with foresight or hindsight.

I can answer "Yes, I see" or "Sorry, I don't see" and ask, "Do you see?" the same way as any sighted person. I can visualize the future. I can be insightful. I can gaze inwardly. I can eyeball a concept. I can keep an idea in my sights. I can *see* others for who they really are more clearly when my eyes are closed.

Looking, eyeing, observing, ogling, watching, beholding, and viewing are concepts I manage with ease. I can imagine but most importantly of all, I can listen. "Hello" I called out loud. "Leonardo, are you still there? I miss you."

He was gone. And it was obvious that silence was infinitely quieter in the dark.

After the 'Tobias' game progressed to an auditory track, I heard the sharp yapping of a mongrel throughout the house or from far off down the beach more often. I called out 'suit yourself then' when it grew silent. But I listened more intently and checked out every scratch and scritch I heard.

I couldn't be sure if the scratching of impatient paws at the door was a demand to be let in or out.

I shone a powerful flashlight in the general direction of canine sounds, half expecting to reveal a trail of muddy pawprints that ended underneath the painting. What was even more absurd... I detected grains of sand in my bed. For someone who can't *see* grit, it's considerably easier to *feel* it. It turned out; a painted dog is much more visible than one that isn't there.

The first thing I did on waking, was rush to examine the 'Tobias'.

This morning Leonardo's charming dog was there. Her button eyes engaged me. She blinked and sneezed when I shone light in her face. She circled the angel and ran off with a yelp. I sensed her sniffing around the Findhorn Box.

We speak now. She confirmed her gender as female.

I began talking to the snuffling sounds that accompanied me throughout the cottage. "If you're here to stay, I suppose I'll have to give you a real name, young lady," I said. And here's where it got weird.

Her voice in my head answered, "My name is Vespers." Imagine a gruff high-pitched Italian voice, and you will have the sense of it.

The word vespers conjured up the poem by A.A. Milne about Christopher Robin saying his prayers. *'I shut my eyes, and I curl up small, and nobody knows that I'm there at all.'* How perfectly blind was that.

Further investigation revealed 'vespers' to be the Latin translation for evening. I had an evening dog who sometimes accompanied me in the mornings and afternoon walks on the beach. "But you're an Italian dog," I said in her direction. "You should be named Sera, that's evening in Italian." And so, I called my evening dog, Sarah. Besides… Sarah means princess and she was definitely, that.

With apologies to the ghost of A.A. Milne, I paraphrased his vespers poem in my diary: *'Little dog curls at the foot of the bed. Hush! Hush! Whisper who dares! Stella and Sarah are saying their prayers.'*

Although being haunted by a canine apparition might frighten some, I was strangely elated not to be alone. Sarah reconnected me to Leonardo and although it wasn't enough, it was a link to the time I had a great friend who loved me.

I knew I was hooked when I couldn't hear the sea because I was intently listening for Sarah.

If one disregards small lap dogs tendency to yap they speak no evil. I hear nothing evil; I can see no evil. An enchanted painting is nothing untoward for me. Playful art is rare. People tend to take art too seriously. In its day, the 'Tobias' was a narrative painting for illiterate worshippers who not only couldn't read but had never held a book.

Apart from religious icons, paintings were comic books for the masses. Pictures dominated. As the first cartoons, the biblical adventures of a boy and his dog bypassed the written word. Memorized text and powerful myths conveyed an everyday lesson of divine intervention.

That thought took hold of me, a non-religious creature who once, and now *almost* believed in magic. This from me who talks to paintings without shame and once held conversations with Leonardo da Vinci on a regular basis. Michael was right. I was a puzzle.

Eccentricity cannot be forced or coerced. A good reporter must be an artful dodger when roaming inner worlds. Once, to be playful, I set a place for Leonardo at dinner. We chatted over invisible spaghetti Bolognese and Coke a Cola which set my guest's nose burning from carbonated burps. Far from being angry, Leonardo was intrigued, guzzled more Coke, and seemed quite disappointed when the soda pop failed to deliver a nasal shock. He was a conundrum. We were twins of a feather.

I freely asked my muses, artists long since passed into history, deeply personal questions in private heart-to-hearts and dreamed their answers. In this way, I kept a toehold on the Italian renaissance, where I should have been born if Madame Superwoman had been on her game.

Had I been born in the fifteenth century, I fancy I would have written a 'history of the artists' that would have blown Giorgio Vasari's feeble pack of lies out of the Arno.

My private confessional would document intimate musings rather than wild theories – a scandal sheet to out-gossip the headlines of quattrocento supermarket tabloids. And should madness be my next and last unsettling phase, I have an immortal companion, presumably loyal to the end, as dogs are wont to be. My doctor may have a point. But that said, being at the bottom of a list for a seeing-eye dog, may have created an anticipated companion. I decided to accept whatever showed up.

CHAPTER 10 - 'SARAH & ME'

It's life's illusions I recall…
I really don't know clouds at all.

'Both Sides, Now' - Joni Mitchel

All day Sarah's untrimmed claws scuttle around me like a restless crab. I trip over her when she sleeps sprawled on the cool Linoleum. No mean feat, pun intended.

I ask myself, if one supernatural event turned into a butterfly effect, could transcendental enlightenment be far behind?

The voice answered before I could take a breath:

"Yes, it absolutely can. But it won't."

I was vexed. "You seem awfully sure."

"I'm always sure. I'm your inner vision. Insight is my business. I suggest you reread your astrology chart. Enlightenment is no 'where' in sight."

"I don't live by the stars anymore."

"Do you not? Well, you might have told me."

"I sense a distinct blip of divine light on my horizon."

"Peripheral vision is tricky to interpret. I shall keep an eye out and keep you informed."

Lucky me.

This morning, Sarah was gone from the painting, which meant

she was busy and would be with me that night. Throughout the day, I experienced breathless excitement at the possibility of an unearthly visitation that had come to stay. A rush of excitement tickled my hopes. I smiled at the childish response I whispered into the painting: "See you later, Sarah," and added "come back soon" to the deserted space where Leonardo's little dog waxed and waned like the phases of the moon.

Assuming ancient mythology is correct, the moon is as feminine as Madame Universe. I take comfort from the notion that Goddesses like Aphrodite, Hera, and Gaia tend to stick together in sisterhoods, covens, coffee klatches, and tea parties.

Whenever I place the tip of my index finger on Sarah's appointed space the gentle snuffling of a dog vibrates inside my body. I feel protected. I am no longer alone. The moon over my island is full. A full moon formed above the horizon. I saw it as a pale blue cloud, and it was enough.

There's always divine light at the end of near-death tunnels, mine included. I say this confidently because, as astral travellers are aware, a cautionary tale contains hidden secrets, and special drawbacks if one is 'out of body' when a magic fish makes you an offer you can't refuse.

Vespers told me her name the first night we met. When I say *told*, I mean she communicated with me telepathically. Her doggy jaws formed no words. She smiled in that endearing way dogs grin with their tongues hanging out. Sarah is versatile. She also smiles with her ears.

She used to clown around to amuse Leonardo by running in circles and falling down. Happy circles appear to be identical to frenzied ones meant to warn me.

Once she materialized, Sarah was a chatterbox. I learned she had been a real dog in Andrea Verrocchio's studio – a resident ratter to curtail the rodent population. Whenever she's missing from the painting, I imagine her off dodging the artists' feet, sniffing for vermin, skittering in time to the sounds of a busy studio, and posing for Leonardo who spoiled her with food so he could sketch her.

Man's best friend became my 'greater' dog. I learned to speak 'cloud dog' fluently.

CHAPTER 11 - **OBEDIENCE SCHOOL**

Star light, star bright,
First star I see tonight
I wish I may, I wish I might,
Have the wish I wish tonight

Sarah was my devoted spirit guide. She kept me on my toes by whining her instructions and relentlessly scratching at the Findhorn Box when it was time for me to meditate. We were a crack team – the newly visible leading the almost blind. I became Sarah's star pupil in accord with Leonardo's creed: *a good student surpasses their teacher.*

The 'Tobias' is a bright narrative. In contrast, my story was fast becoming a pastel of watery colors bleached in the heat of August.

As a smug art student, I had autopsied this multi-flawed work to discern if there'd been a competent overseer. I'd concluded, not. Likely, the composition, once established by Master Verrocchio, had grown somewhat like a mushroom in a dark side-chamber away from the constant hustle of business – the regular standing orders for mass produced terracotta saints and Madonnas that paid the studio's bills.

The Italian renaissance reduced to today's system of profit and loss never failed to surprise me.

I'd never considered the full narrative connection of Tobias's parable with the studio's history. Wild goose chases aside, an archangel blindly leading a child on a supernatural road to happiness was relatively predictable for a bible story.

Sarah informed me there was a parallel story. A surprise I needed to know. She promised to tell me when it was the right time. I became a little unnerved when she added "You'll have to remain calm for anything to work properly. Do you understand? You'll have to comply with my demands as I have done with yours. What will you do, I wonder, when I tell *you* to roll over and play dead, hmmnn?"

A fifteenth-century spirit dog should have been enough to freak me out, but with my dodgy future, supernatural advice was expected. By her own admission, Sarah's storytelling is magical, akin to performance art. She tends to exaggerate, so, I didn't believe her, but what Sarah eventually showed me was heavy-duty hocus-pocus from the business end of a magic wand.

Sarah made it her duty to 'see me through' the boring part first: I had no choice but to play by her rules.

Once upon a time, a man fell asleep in the sun, and while he was sleeping a bird pecked at his eyes causing inflammation, a fever, and eventual blindness. Times were hard. The family had no income. But the father remembered a man in a far-off city who owed him a considerable sum of money. And so, he ordered his son, Tobias, to make his way there and retrieve the funds.

But since the roads were unsafe for a boy travelling alone, the father bid his son to find a man from their village as a guide.

The local men were superstitious and refused to help, believing Tobias's father's blindness was a curse, but a stranger in the tavern approached the boy and offered his services as he was headed the same direction. And so, they set off. Tobias's faithful dog had no intention of being left behind and trotted after them.

A terrifying encounter with a giant magic fish when crossing a river, unnerved Tobias. Tobias, fearful of drowning, had grabbed its tail and was towed to shore, only to discover the landed monster was a non-threatening modest sized fish.

It was welcomed as a fortuitous gift of supper, tied to a string, and carried towards the city of prosperity, jiggling like a marionette.

And so, the journey continued.

An hour later, Tobias and his guide arrived at the walls of a great city where Tobias collected his father's money with all due speed. And much to Tobias's surprise, the stranger showed himself to be the Angel Raphael. Raphael prepared the little fish into a medicinal paste and Tobias was bid to return home in all haste and apply it to his father's eyes.

I dismissed the storyline even though its theme of blindness unnerved me, cutting terribly close to the bone. But instead of exhibiting anxiety, I gave Sarah a spattering of applause more in tune with my anticipation of the bigger surprise to come.

I might have known there'd be a caveat. By definition, a show dog must show off. It seems I had to earn the right to partake of Sarah's theatrical third act, which meant it would take time and effort to prove my worthiness. A piece of Dundee cake. No problem.

Spiritual training began in earnest. Meditation lowered my blood pressure and I learned to use a white cane. I was a natural. Sarah put me through my paces, forever underfoot and moving to test me, the art of paying attention to peripheral vision being the key to success. I also made my peace with a newfangled machine that recorded speech into printed words.

I dictated a new essay on Leonardo's apprenticeship related to 'The Angel and Tobias' commission, faxed it to my doctor's office, to be returned in braille. I couldn't read the thing, but it turned out to be a tactile form of meditation. I ran the tips of my fingers lightly over the small hills and valleys, and lumps and bumps, and concentrated, listening for words to appear in my mind, on the principle that believing is seeing.

But I was concerned. As my eyesight faded in the highs and lows of a temperamental dimmer switch, Sarah lost density. It was only a matter of time before she permanently disappeared like the 'Last Supper' and I would be left alone, dangling helplessly as a marionette fish with cut strings.

All things considered, my advice was to never take 2020 vision for granted, never look a gift-fish in the mouth, and always keep a watchful eye, even a dodgy one, for a light on the horizon. Listen with your eyes and if you have an energized touchstone, pay attention to it with every fibre of your being.

CHAPTER 12- **NO END IN SIGHT**

'The Hippopotamus Song'
1960 – Flanders & Swann

I may be going crazy. Not from talking to a phantom dog but talking to a phantom 'Mother'.

Madame Universe is misbehaving. I didn't expect her to be a vicious 'agony aunt' with a taste for revenge, which goes to show I know next to nothing about divine intervention. Though I have to say, a little compassion wouldn't go amiss.

It's disconcerting when some days my Goddess Mother takes on the persona of a witchy hag casting toxic spells like chickenfeed. But once-in-a-while, to keep me guessing, Milady was kindness itself.

I wished for more such days.

I came to accept I'd been born at an inopportune time under a malefic star. But there wasn't a *single* problem with such a clear directive; there was an *overabundance* of problems.

At first hearing, *overabundance* sounds quite positive. More abundance must surely be, pardon the expression, a godsend. It was not. It was a hellbent curse. It made me wonder how many prayers went astray from incorrect terminology.

For the most part, I sat with my pain in silence. But eyestrain headaches were a power unto themselves. They swarmed like bees, attacked like a sky full of crows divebombing a single crust of bread, and pecked at one's eyes with the fury of starving vultures.

Sarah, a child dog, once invisible and audible, advanced to the Victorian ideal of being unseen *and* heard to assist me. She was a devoted empath, instinctively understanding her high-pitched yelp was doing my head in and softened it to a canine sigh.

Which brings me to my grievances with dear old Mum in an open letter:

Dear all-seeing Mama –
I left you in an emotional quandary as a teenager, but now, with the best of intentions, I've returned to square one consciousness. 'Spirituality 101' commands me to accept what-is. *Whatever* it is. I've filled notebooks with affirmations. I've made lists and drawn storyboards. I've meditated and repeated mantras.

The trouble is, deep down, I don't believe a word of them. I'm a frightened parrot spewing empty platitudes. Giving in sounds easy but it's not. Surrender is a grand idea but it's hard work, and the pretence of lying to the universe with my fingers crossed behind my back is just bad form.

I'm beyond angry. I *don't* accept what-is. I DON'T WANT TO BE BLIND! There, I've said it. Please believe me, I don't mean to sound arrogant or false. I'm not as unreasonable as I used to be. But I'm in the dark, here. Pun intended.

Some things we both know to be true. For years you've heard me rabbiting on in a pity party of my own creation about the perils of accidental birth. We both know I took the art of wallowing to a new dimension. But something fresh has been added to my repertoire. I've changed.

Sarah has opened my eyes. I've taken to heart every loving philosophy that ever fell to earth in a shower of falling stars. The asteroid that killed the dinosaurs may have a distant cousin because I've felt it approaching most of my life. It was coming for me. I froze in fear. And now, I stand firm at ground zero ready to take the full impact as a penance worthy of a petulant child.

I don't expect to go unscathed. Perhaps unsightly spectacles with insanely strong lenses would be enough. In theory, I embrace the idea of surgery and if diminished vision comes, I will face that too. I think you'll agree that faking courage like this is a form of true bravery, although on second thought, a pair of *unsightly* spectacles seems redundant.

But irony often speaks louder than words. It's not like I'm *refusing* to be blind. Nothing of the sort. Blindness happens. There's no point in denying such a fact. If fighting anything is bad, then so is fighting the good fight. Resistance is asking for trouble, and you know I've had my share. I get that my eyesight is fading by the day. I understand the physical dynamics of the thing. Retinas and optical nerves are demanding body parts. Things burn out. But I must speak as I find. With all the humility I can rally, I have a serious question. You might even say it's a *Sirius* question.

Madame Universe, Great Earth Mother, Gaia. Milady, Dearest Mama, I didn't lie to you when I promised to serve you. I invited you into my life as a friend. Spiritual teachings told me to do that, too. It was painless. Some sentiments are easier than others. So, my question is this: with all due respect, shouldn't spirituality feel more… spiritual?

Because I see stars. Fuzzy out of focus stars. Shooting stars behind my eyes. Painful comets with fiery tails penetrate my brain. No disrespect intended, but my headaches are so incredibly intense I've begun to pray for real. I've considered going to church; I've considered exorcism; I've considered jumping out a window.

I accept the fact that meditation is meant to be silent contemplation, but I prefer to communicate with you by speaking plainly in real time. Audio visual works for me. I'm desperate, and as desperate as that sounds, I have accepted 'what-is' in the loosest definition of acceptance that I can… well, accept.

I'm seeing impossible things through muddied water. You'd think that seeing anything would be a good, considering the alternative, but chaotic visions distract me from the peace I've found with Sarah. A continual warning runs like tickertape behind my eyes: *'mad dogs and Englishmen go out in the noonday sun.'* Well, here I am… a mad Englishwoman. Mad as in angry, yet 'barking mad' is not entirely off the table, and Sarah howls down the moon every evening as her prime duty. Please help us.

Flashing auras erase half of everything I can still see, and I can no longer read even with a hand over one eye. I can't tell if I'm dreaming or awake anymore.

Furniture vibrates into excited electrons and comes and goes. Starfish twinkle in a Van Gogh sky on my ceiling. Vincent's wild stripes undulate across it like the aurora borealis on speed. My walls a.k.a. projector screens run back-to-back movies of amoebas wriggling under a microscope. Small worries scuttle under my bed and climb the chintz curtains where they pluck the roses and scatter petals over me in a snowstorm of pink flakes.

The real eye-opener is tinnitus. Circus music loops non-stop, from a kaleidoscopic insane asylum that has taken up residence in my brain. My head rattles with bits of broken glass that rotate into a mindscape of shattered stained-glass windows. Beautiful but there's no off button.

Shadow people arrive at my bedside moving fast as keystone cops: pirates in costume, ballerinas wearing space helmets, and schools of flying fish. Sometimes Tobias's fish is alone, riding a white horse. Sometimes the pirates spin like ballerinas.

Meditating makes me dizzy, so much so it feels like wool-gathering from the back seat of a moving car. But whenever I rise above thought, a shapeless blob grabs me by the ankles and pulls me down to earth. Meditation's celestial twin, navel-gazing, is no better. Motion sickness rules: the romantic notion of swinging on a star amounts to vertigo on a high trapeze.

The hallucinations are annoying; the pain behind my eyes is excruciating; the suffering is cruel. Please make it stop. If blindness is the only way to open my heart, I beg you to take the light from me and bring on the dark in all due haste. And Mom, I thank you for Sarah. Truly, I do.

May I respectfully suggest, it might be *your* turn to accept *me* as I am.

It's not like I'm asking for the sun, the moon, and the stars… just to turn a blind eye from one little star before, heaven forfend, it goes nova.

Bark if you can hear me!

The next night I had another Leonardo dream. I visited Verrocchio's studio and watched Leonardo create Vespers as a drawing in sepia ink on heavy paper. But the drawing wasn't right, and so I whispered a solution in Leonardo's ear. He took fresh paper and Vespers returned slightly smaller in scale. I patted Leonardo on the back and kissed his cheek. He smiled and rubbed the kiss, leaving a smear of charcoal.

I'm familiar with the transfer process. Leonardo took a sharpened stick and made a continuous line of holes following the outline of his drawing. He positioned it on the panel, pounded charcoal dust into the pin holes, and pulled away the paper to reveal a black outline. What remained looked like a constellation. A black dog star! My friend is a genius.

Leonardo connected the stars with a fine brush dipped in yellow ochre oil paint, and indicated the precise position of Vespers' nose, but he placed her eyes too far apart.

Just then, a child servant bringing food, tripped over the real Vespers. The boy broke his fall with his hands, landing directly onto the wet paint.

Vespers' eyes were smeared beyond repair. She snuffled softly as Leonardo tenderly wiped them away and replaced them the perfect distance apart. Vespers' expression was true. Her eyes were brighter… they smiled. Her paws pranced lighter on the road; a summer breeze ruffled the feathery curls of her fur.

Vespers has haunted the 'Tobias' for ages. Her ghostly form has clung precariously in situ for 500 years. Her creator, Leonardo is a superstar.

I wake with *my* own dear Sarah licking my eyelids.

CHAPTER 13 – **THE DARKEST HOUR**

Wm. Shakespeare
- 'A Midsummer Night's Dream'

The end came fast.

I was sitting in a chair when the floor disappeared. The walls and ceiling followed. The world was gone. I reached down, pulled on a slipper, and slithered an invisible nightgown over my head. Sarah brought me the missing slipper.

I crawled towards the bathroom and stood squinting into a ceramic cave.

I pretended I was wearing a blindfold and inched zombie-like towards the sound of draining bathwater. My fingers gripped the cold lip of the bathroom sink, and I drew myself up to face the blank mirror.

I splashed cold tap water on my face and hid behind a towel before I dared take a second look.

For an awkward moment, the left side of my face shimmered there like a crescent moon. Half a ghost stared back at me.

My right eye manifested for a second and blinked out.

My senses came on board. I smelled soap, water gurgled down

the drain, and I peered into the mirror until the tip of my nose touched the glass. My lips moved and my voice echoed back as a magic spell. 'Mirror mirror on the wall who's the fairest of them all?'

"Get a grip, princess," the mirror replied.

I let go of the sink and patted my leg. "Sarah, come here, sweetheart."

Sarah scampered over to me and pawed my legs.

I dropped on all fours. Sarah licked my face and ran in circles around me, yapping madly. The scent of her fur was strong. I recognized turpentine and vinegar. "Take me to the bed there's a luv," I said, and amazingly, she obeyed.

In no time, I pulled myself up by the footboard and collapsed on my back, arms spreadeagled on the bedspread. Sarah pranced playfully, tugging the sleeve of my nightdress.

I cuddled Sarah under a bedspread tent and lost consciousness or at least I slept deeply for an indeterminate time.

The realization that I would never again know what time it was came as a shock. World events would play out as radio news. My feeble comings and goings would stumble along in a series of best guesses. But at least I would never have to read a newspaper horoscope again. My '*horror*-scope' linked to a treacherous star fell to earth with a thud vaporizing the last dinosaur bone inside me.

I covered my ears but the ticking heart inside my head boomed louder, pounding with pulsating blood. I visualized my brain as a clock – a cuckoo clock that would crow madly, forever marking the hours and half hours – a clockwork woman fumbling in the dark – an empress at the head of a public procession wearing no clothes. Their laughter already mocked me from afar.

Sarah's bark sounded inside my head; hot tears stung my useless eyes. I clawed at them in a fury, pointlessly defacing the face the world would see.

The blind spot in the bathroom mirror was like looking down a dark tunnel, yet I knew, somewhere miles away, I was behind the looking glass, waving a white flag.

"Surrender everything," a voice said.

"I'm experiencing night terrors," I whined.

"Surrender."

"But I've been erased."

"Nonsense. You've been edited. Satori is as satori does. Put your fears into perspective, child. Now you see them; now you don't. Don't you know it's poetic to dematerialize before your very own eyes."

"I'm not a child."

"Then stop acting like one."

"Am I still here?"

"Of course, you bloody are. Can you not feel your teeth with your tongue?"

I found the toothpaste, brushed the empty space I knew my

teeth to be and rinsed my mouth with warm water. Suddenly, I felt alone. Frantic. Had Sarah gone too?

Sarah's wet nose pressed into my leg.

"Tsk. Such a fuss over one little night terrier," the voice said.

CHAPTER 14 – **SATORI**

Summertime… and the livin' is easy
Fish are jumpin' and the cotton is high
So hush, little baby, don't you cry

Summertime – Johnny Hodges

AUGUST 11, 2022 –

THE 'DOG DAYS OF SUMMER' END

Sarah's enthusiasm for my company made up for my diminished senses. She provided sounds for me to follow but I wondered if a small dog could guide me to a more forgiving star. Sarah barked "Easy peasy". I hoped it was so.

As a fluffy touchstone, she grounded me with loving companionship. She wriggled into the crook of my arm at bedtime, sighing and gently snoring. She snuffled and scratched and panted in a language I understood and barked me awake like an alarm clock. Her cold nose, warm tongue, and body heat consoled me. We consoled each other.

An invisible umbilical cord between us acted as a leash. Her energy tugged me forward and around stumbling blocks. I trusted her eyes implicitly. She taught me how to maneuver obstacles and paths fraught with pitfalls of uneven terrain and clumps of tripping thatch grass, broken seashells, and sharp rocks. I pictured where I wanted to go, donned a blindfold to train my ears, and Sarah led me there.

All our meals were picnics, taken at odd times of the day, or well into the sunset, and under the stars.

The golden aura of my phantom seeing-eye dog shone luminescent in the dark like a glowing candle. In the daylight, Sarah was transparent as gauze. I literally 'saw through' her tricks. At night, she radiated love as a ball of excited light, always showing her true-blue colors.

My sight failed simultaneously with Sarah's disappearance. In my darkest hour, she pulled me towards the painting. The last I saw of her was a blurry bundle of fluff leaping inside it. Sarah howled a goodbye from within the frame and was gone.

"Sarah, come! I commanded, but all I heard was muffled yelping from far away followed by silence.

I finally groped my way to the bed and removed my blindfold but as I slipped beneath the covers, I felt Sarah's weight on my legs, raking my blankets in a state of urgency.

She nipped my toe, growling and carrying on for me to follow her, until I stood facing the 'Tobias' a shape I could barely make out by squinting. Slowly, Sarah's form materialized on the road, my bedroom dissolved into a sunny Italian day, and I was inside the painting.

Raphael took my arm. "There you are," he said. "We must hurry. You have a long way to go. There's not much time."

The landscape came into focus bursting under a brilliant azure sky with lemon groves reaching for miles either side. I drank in the smell of linseed oil and fresh paint that wafted over me.

Leonardo's jewellike fish winked slyly. Tobias handed me its string and disappeared.

Raphael and I walked down a path lined with strangely shaped rocks and tufts of turquoise seagrass. I stared ahead and spoke as if I was alone. "Why am I here? Raphael, I know who you are. At least I know what the mythologies say. You protect the blind. Are you going to save my eyes? Is that even possible?"

The road disappeared and I panicked. "I fear it may be too late," Raphael replied. "You're a dogged woman. Fear is your specialty."

It was then I discovered angels were irritating mind readers. "Roads are illusions," Raphael went on. "At this moment we are walking down the *thought* of a road made from ground pigments, egg yolks and vinegar water." He kicked a stone that resembled a poached egg. "You see, another bad egg. This entire painted world is eggs. I think the stones are following us."

A couple of the 'poached rocks' zoomed off ahead of us. "Or leading us," I replied. "I shouldn't be here. I'm flesh and blood."

Raphael stared distractedly into the botched sky. "Is Sarah flesh and blood?"

I bent down and touched Sarah's fur, hot from the sun. Her tongue scratched my hand.

"I can feel her."

"But can *she* feel *you*?"

I cried then and turned back the way we'd come, hoping the painting was still a door to my bedroom. But I remained solidly trapped in a flat colorless scene. The landscape and Tobias were barely charcoal outlines sketched on a familiar white panel prepared with gesso.

I assumed I must be a two-dimensional hostage. The angel had taken everything physical from me. Perhaps he'd taken my soul. Perhaps I had died. Perhaps Sarah had deserted me.

Tobias stood frozen – a cardboard cut-out wearing a quizzical expression. I held out the exquisite marionette fish to tempt him, but he was blind to my presence.

Raphael rattled the small pillbox he was carrying in my face. It made no sound. "Gallbladders are quiet," he said. "Livers and hearts too. But they aren't in this box. Not *yet*. This box is empty. You might say it's my miniature Findhorn Box. Inside are the thoughts of firecracker stars believing they're radioactive mud and gas." He tossed it in the air, caught it without looking on the tip of his finger, and presented it to me. "The night sky is in here," he said. "Trust is in here. The dog star is in here. Would you care to see it?"

I refused, somewhat offended. "No thanks, I may be blind, but

I can see you're not to be trusted."

My rudeness broke the spell. Sarah sneezed, Tobias animated in full color, and Sarah jumped into my arms all squirmy and real.

Raphael chuckled. "Just a quick hello, then? for old time's sake?"

I gave my angel a look one saves for devils.

"Then for heaven's sake, say goodbye to the past," Raphael said. "And make it count. You know you want to. But all will be as it was. Your salvation lies at the end of this road. But it's your choice. It always has been."

Sarah jumped at the fish, now dancing like a puppet with scales that smelled of violets.

Raphael's musical laughter enchanted me. "My child, if you *believe* fish smell like violets, therein lies the crux of your problem. You BELIEVE you are blind. And why should you not. Your symptoms indicate a reduced ability to see. This is the suffering hard won from unrestrained fear. And believe me, it's not easy to feel that much fear at once. But you possess infinite powers. So farsighted are you, you're nearsighted. So insightful, you've chosen to fear everything before it happens, and this *everything* has progressed to metaphysical blindness. Do you see?"

"Why would you ask such a cruel question?"

"Because child… it is the *only* question."

"Why would I pretend such a thing?"

"Humans pretend all the time," Raphael said. He turned to Tobias, restored to life dangling the fish over Sarah's head, as 3-dimensional as you like. Tobias's painted mouth grinned. His painted shoulders shrugged. "Your vision is so boundlessly unframed you see nothing," Raphael said. The fish winked. Its tail flipflopped and its watery voice gurgled in my head *'no need to thank me'* it said. *'But I need you to do me a wee favor.'*

I was so shocked I narrowly missed tripping over a stone that resembled a miniature flying saucer with legs, but it scuttled away sideways like a crab.

"It's time for a rest," Raphael said at last. He led me into the grass, gently pushed me into a seated position and proceeded to massage my dusty toes. "Stella my angel, you have done well."

Sarah fidgeted in my lap as Raphael chopped the fish's innards into paste, ground them into a fine ointment, and scraped the goo of it into a bowl that looked an awful lot like my singing bowl. "I hope you don't mind me borrowing this," Raphael said. "It seemed appropriate. Maybe now is the perfect time to talk about your dream. Or was the Leonardo dream that haunted you so many years ago a nightmare? Thirty-six if I'm not mistaken."

I studied the intricate embroidery of Raphael's sleeve until I was cross-eyed. "I thought I saw…"

"Aha! You *did* see something. I knew it!"

"No. Please, allow me to rephrase. I *imagined* I saw something."

"And the difference is?"

"Huge… thinking and pretending are worlds apart. Reality and fantasy can never meet. I don't believe in miracles. But then, I always failed to believe I was worthy!"

Raphael's eyes narrowed.

My eyes closed tight. "Okay, okay. If I'm honest, I *felt* something in my dream that's too embarrassing to explain."

"All in good time, little one. Tell me when you're ready."

While Raphael worked, I entertained him with a story about my grandmother's specialty, 'Stargazy Pie' - a deep dish of pilchards baked whole, peering skyward through holes cut in the pastry crust. I couldn't stomach the sight of forlorn little fish captured in a pie, but I'd shut my eyes and ate it to please my grandmother.

"It sounds heavenly," Raphael said. "You used your eyes rightly when you were a child. No blind spots until… well, not to put too fine a point on it, until Findhorn and that star debacle."

"You know," I said. "Unlike you, humans make mistakes. When I saw the 'Tobias' by the stairs, I thought you must be an advanced time traveller as the little box you were carrying looked like a cell phone."

Raphael shook his head so vehemently his Frisbee halo floated loose. "The traveller was always Leonardo and a close associate of his who has always kept an eye on you."

Sarah sneezed and barked at the same time and rolled over.

Raphael laughed. "Many a true word is sneezed in jest," he said, rewarding Sarah with a morsel of fish. He patted the top of her head. "Clever girl." He put her through her paces. "Sit! Stay! Heel! Roll over! Now, please show Stella how to play dead!"

We resumed our journey and in no time at all we came to a walled city where Sarah led us through a tall gate. She barked madly, and Raphael gently nudged me forward.

I found myself alone, staring down a dank tunnel. I smelled the sea ahead of me and walked towards the sounds of seagulls and crashing waves.

The bedclothes were still rumpled in my bedroom. I lurched to the bed, arms outstretched holding a bowl of goo, and climbed in. I felt for the blindfold I'd abandoned on my pillow, dipped it into the ointment, and covered my eyes with a poultice that smelled like the lemon groves of Fiesole.

When I awoke, the contents of the room were painted with sunlight. I touched objects as if for the first time: a smoothed lump of ultramarine sea glass shaped like a poached egg, a gritty sand dollar, and Michael's listening stone that stirred in my hand emitting red sparks from its speckled iron inclusions. The painting was gone; Sarah was gone; my sight had returned.

I had no time to grieve Sarah's loss as the sound of crunching gravel announced the approach of a car. From the window I recognized my doctor's Mercedes. I clamped on my sunglasses, grabbed the white cane, and took the stairs two at a time, calling Sarah all the way.

A plaintive farewell inside my head whined back *'I love you. Look for me. I'm always with you – out of sight; always in your mind. Forever in your heart. Thank you, my brave Stella. Brava!'*

The car door opened, and a blonde stranger alighted, waving hello. "Special delivery," he called out. "Your doctor sent me with your seeing-eye dog. He wanted to surprise you."

I faked blindness behind my designer shades and tapped my way forward as a small terrier jumped from the back seat, trailing a leash. I wanted to shout *'well aren't you a sight for sore eyes'*, but I stopped in time, remembering I wasn't supposed to see her. I had no intention of losing her twice.

Sarah pranced a little but settled down to the *'sirius'* business of a trained guide dog. I bent down and hugged her until she squirmed her old wild way. The fish-shaped tag on her collar, read, Toby.

The trainer and I shook hands. "Her name is Toby," he said in a familiar voice. "She's a champion. Chosen for her loyalty. You should thank your lucky stars for her." When he placed the leash in my hand and squeezed my arm, a spark of energy woke my body. His parting words were delivered with a wink. "Well, I'll leave you two to get acquainted."

As he turned towards the car, a gust of wind blew sand between us. When it settled the car was gone and the stranger revealed his true form. He wore richly embroidered robes, red sandals, and carried a halo on his arm like a bracelet. And as he continued to walk away, wings sprouted from his back. A whirlwind fog spiraled around him. Toby barked and Raphael vanished.

Back inside the kitchen, the painting was nowhere to be found. Toby and I breakfasted on microwave-bacon sandwiches and headed for the beach.

I strolled barefoot, my sunglasses pushed to the top of my head, face upturned to catch the sun, twirling the white cane like Charlie Chaplin. I sang a line from his song 'Smile' to honor him and my new life: *'you know that life can be worthwhile if you just smile.'*

Toby ran ahead and found a crab to sniff. I took in the cloudless powder-blue sky, remembered to thank my lucky stars twice, and kept a watchful eye on the horizon for pirate ships. A squadron of airplanes droned overhead but the aquamarine sky was bereft of dog fights. We ventured further down the beach into forbidden territory, clambering over the dangerous boulders I so recently had to avoid.

There, in a deep windbreak of stone slabs was the painting, glass intact, leaning against a rock face. When Toby barked frantically at the painting, Vespers, inside, animated and leapt at the glass scratching to get out. For a few minutes, two dogs separated by glass revelled in a barking match, but Tobias whistled. Vespers ran in a circle a few times, whined through her nose, and obediently rejoined her master.

The angel, Tobias, and Vespers continued their journey and walked out of view. When Vespers' muffled barks faded into silence, the empty road morphed into a narrow strip of sand. The landscape disappeared in the pop of a flashbulb that silvered the picture glass into a mirror. I took it home and hung it in its old place.

As I stood back to straighten it, my reflection caught my eye. *"There you are!"* it said. *"I thought it was you."*

CHAPTER 15 – **TIME OF DEATH**

I surfaced from a deeply sensuous dream, squinting into the silent half-light of evening. Moonbeams were still painting my furniture pale lavender blue. All was still until I felt a weight on my feet. Toby kneaded the covers grinning at me like a fluorescent Cheshire dog in the dark.

I tried to shake her off. More than life itself I wanted to return to one of the most wonderful dreams of my life. Toby's demanding bark hit my spine like a jolt of electricity.

"Bad dog," I shouted and wished I hadn't.

I rose from my bed against my will, landed lightly on my feet, and headed for the door. But a warning growl from Toby made me turn around. I saw myself still in bed struggling for breath.

I closed my eyes and looked again. I was smiling. I looked away, shocked, and dared to look again. I no longer struggled. My breaths came in shallow inhales and contented exhales. I rattled my last with Toby licking my hand.

When it was over the room was brighter. Toby clowned around me in excited circles. "Come on," she said clearly.

"Leonardo is waiting. And please call me Sarah."

"And why would Leonardo care?"

"You'd be surprised how much you're revered," she said.

"Nothing would surprise me more."

"Follow me," Sarah whined with more urgency. "It's best we go *now*. You don't have to watch what happens next. I don't want you upset. Humans are far too connected to their bodies."

"There's no need to protect me. I'm a big girl."

"Have you seen yourself lately? Do the words 'time of death' have any special meaning to you?"

"I am the late Stel…"

"Yes, yes, I know. You're making wise with words. Leonardo loved to do that."

The word 'late' echoed away like the receding tide.

Sarah gave an impassioned howl. "Look at yourself. You're outside your body. Death is a new sensation. You may as well get used to new sensations."

"By the looks of my feet, I'm a teenager, again."

"Weren't you always?"

"Momento," I said speaking Italian with ease, covering my final smile with the bedsheet. Taking leave of the bedside felt like hello rather than goodbye… I sent a hopeful *see you soon* to my lifeless body. *Next life we'll do better,* I promised.

A red beeper flashed from my body's exposed wrist indicating an emergency code had activated. I would be rescued. No…

never rescued, retrieved.

My body felt light as a helium balloon. It could have easily floated off by itself. Another engaging sensation. I was eager for more.

The voice of one of the medics shouting to the other, interrupted us. "I think the old dear may have had a dog; we'd better have a look around."

Medic One scribbled a grim notation in his report: *estimated time of death: 2 a.m.* "Give or take," he said setting aside the clipboard, and proceeded to look under the sofa and check the closets.

Medic Two went outside and called over the dunes banging a dish with a spoon. They met on the front porch for a new plan when a plaintive bark issued from the kitchen. Medic Two jumped into action. "There it is. Good. We need to get out of here before the tide comes in. I hope it's not a vicious guard dog or one of those little snappy ones. I'm not keen on dogs. A goldfish will do me."

There WAS a dog. A red chalk study of Vespers lay on the table. Its rough handmade paper, yellowed and brittle from age, was recognizable as the pose used in the 'Tobias'. I'd seen it in my dream when I was seventeen, witnessing Leonardo's long hours studying her movements and observed him sketching and playing with his new friend. No detail had been too insignificant to capture: walking, sitting, sleeping; fur damp, soaking wet, or windblown. Leonardo combed Vesper's coat with his fingertips causing it to stand on end and smoothed it flat. He sniffed it on each occasion and made notes. He was nothing if not thorough.

Sepia notations in the margins were easily identifiable as Leonardo's unique mirror writing.

A gentle breeze caught the curled paper and moved it an inch.

Medic One called out. "Did you find it? Do you need any help?"

"I found a *picture* of a dog," Medic Two called back.

Medic One shuffled into the room. "Right, pictures of dogs bark all the time."

"I think it's really old. It's art. You know… *really old*."

"Where is it?"

"On the table."

"*Um*…There's nothing on the table."

"It was there a minute ago."

"Drawings don't disappear. You were hallucinating."

A distant bark came from outside. "I guess the drawing must have walked outside, then."

"This island has a weird reputation. I'm feeling antsy. Take a few pictures of the body before we move it. It's high tide as well as high time, we get out of here."

Sarah and I watched the ambulance take away the body.

Leonardo's drawing faded from the paper which disintegrated

into dust and blew into a corner.

Momentarily, Vesper's essence lay as dust before it was sucked out the open door, taking Toby with it.

Sarah, free to run on our beach, barked from a million miles away in her *'I've cornered something interesting'* bark.

I saw her in my mind's eye pawing frantically at a white butterfly.

When I materialized beside her it flew to my shoulder and rose into what I was sure was a painted egg-tempura sky with some alarmingly clumsy clouds.

Sarah disappeared with the butterfly. I called her. She answered from far down the beach.

Sarah raced towards me, fluffy ears flapping behind her, and jumped into my arms. The new object of her attention was a beached fish, its iridescent scales dried to a brilliant enamel. "I expect I have to say goodbye," I said in a choked voice. "It's time for me to go."

"Where to?" Sarah asked her ears perked in a question mark.

"I'm guessing, *not* heaven," I replied sarcastically.

"I have no earthly idea where that is," she whined.

We took the main dirt road gliding through the low cloud of dust raised by the ambulance. Sarah marched proudly ahead and paused to wait for me whenever I lagged behind. "You do know you can travel with your thoughts in the afterlife," she admonished.

"I'd like to savor the feeling of levitating above the road if you don't mind. Death to bunions and all that. Thought pedicures are so practical."

Suit yourself," Sarah answered. "You always do."

"I didn't want to wake up," I confessed. "You know, back then when I was… you know."

"Dying?"

"Yes, that. It's a difficult concept to accept. I was dreaming of Michael."

"Sometimes waking up takes a lifetime."

"If you say so. I was dreaming of 1986. My first year of art college, besotted over my lovely painter boy. It was the year we fell in love."

"I thought that was the year you became smitten with Leonardo."

"It was. Michael introduced us. I saw Leonardo through his eyes. I loved them both."

Sarah wagged her entire body. "I'll say one positive thing about humans in love; they behave more like dogs."

"Michael and I critiqued every painting and sculpture. He knew so much. And he… oh! Michael introduced me to the 'Tobias'… and you."

"And I was pleased to bark hello, but you didn't hear me."

"I don't understand."

"You were concentrating."

"I was sketching. *You*, as it happens. I tend to get distracted when I draw so I wear headphones. Music centers me."

"And?"

"There was some vague commotion, but I didn't pay much attention. Michael told me later a wee dog had been running loose in the gallery. I remember hearing barking, but I assumed it was my imagination. I was deep into creating a dog of my own… Oh! Was that you?"

"You wish. You're not that powerful… yet. I ran past you several times to Michael's amusement. More than a few patrons heard me. I caused quite a stir. In fact, I still do on occasion. I like to keep my eye on the painting from time-to-time, and I always look for rats and such. Old habits die hard. And speaking of death, there's a bit more to it regarding erratic time fluctuations."

"Those are big words for a little dog," I said.

Sarah growled a warning. "Don't tempt me, Stella. I'm on a mission."

"I remember Michael commenting that Leonardo had just stepped away from his painting, and there we were, arriving a few brushstrokes later."

"My point exactly," Sarah whined. "An erratic fluctuation of time."

My eyes glazed over from the memories of our early courtship. "Michael kissed me that day… as much as we dared in a public place. *"500 years evaporated in a surreal heartbeat,"* he'd whispered between kisses. He was a true romantic."

"Ah, no, that was *me*, evaporating," Sarah bragged.

"I sketched you for Michael as a St. Michael's Day present. Two years later, in Findhorn, I had my astrology chart made for the same holiday. I remember because the astrologer was a plain creature, and she had a bit of a crush on Michael."

"Really? Well, I'd never have guessed."

"Michael knew so much about art."

Sarah barked her *I'm impatient to be off,* bark. "Michael always was a wonder. Now… I'm on a time sensitive schedule," she said. "I promised Leonardo we wouldn't dawdle."

"What's the hurry? From now on I am the late *Stella-what's-her-name*. Art may be immortal, but I am assuredly, not. Where do I go now?"

"It's simple. You come with me. I'm your seeing eye guide dog, remember?"

"And now you're my intrepid tour guide, lead on."

Sarah shook her fur as if she'd been delivered from a bath. "I've been trying to."

"Strange that my last dream would be of Michael. I haven't thought of him in years."

"It only takes one dreamer to keep lovers connected."

"I wonder what became of him. Why on earth did I leave him? He was the love of my life. It makes no sense."

"Well, it *wasn't* written in the stars, that's true and certain. All humans have a blind spot. One maleficent girl… *not* you as it happens… can rule the day. And there are many more senses than six as you will soon discover."

"Was I cruel to Michael?"

"Only to yourself. Which reminds me, I wanted to ask you about your 'Leonardo dream'. You started to tell Raphael you saw something."

"I already told you. I saw myself through Leonardo's eyes."

CHAPTER 16 – **FIRENZE**

"Men, at some time, are masters of their fates.
The fault, dear Brutus, is not in our stars,
But in ourselves,
That we are underlings."

William Shakespeare

I smelled the lemon groves before I saw them. Cypress trees, the elegant signature of Tuscan landscape, lined the road and fields either side like sentries guarding the way to Florence.

We were greeted at a city gate by Gianni, a young serving boy I recognized from the studio who had died young after being cast as a cherub in a pageant. He'd been slathered in gold paint, suspended on pulleys and ropes, forced to hover for hours sweating under a toxic coat and withered away in a feverish malady of unknown origin. His death had been slow and painful.

"No time to waste on sad things," Sarah whined. "Our destination awaits."

"And where is that?"

"Verrocchio's studio," she answered, looking at me as if I was a numpty to even ask.

"Sorry, how? Didn't I just die?"

"Are you barking mad? We're going to *feel* ourselves there," she said. "An alert body is required. You'll get the hang of it."

"Before I go any further with you, I need a few answers."

Sarah prodded me with her cold wet nose. "That won't take long," she said. "Because I know all the questions."

"Fine. I'll just listen to you lecture. Is this the mysterious parallel story you promised to reveal?"

Sarah pawed the floor and settled into a sphinxlike pose. "Not yet but soon I will have to. The deceased are much wiser in the afterlife, Stella. Have you noticed that you and I are telepathically connected?"

"I thought we always were."

"Art history is in the details, dear heart. Most of our early communications were one-way. Mostly speculations on your part. Brain synapses are often too intense to be accurate, but at least they offer the illusion of understanding.

Best pay attention. I shall begin in the middle when you were seventeen years old, and I was 517. As I recall, you were rambling on to some visitor about Leonardo and how my portrait was disappearing like his 'Last Supper', which, by the way, was somewhat accurate but not the whole truth. I barked at your worst mistakes, but you had that contraption over your ears. I sent some facts your way, of course. But Michael did most of the work."

"Michael! Oh my god… Michael was there! I feel strangely… displaced."

"Brava. You're beginning to feel like a ghost. Please pay close attention." Sarah prodded me hard with her nose. "Leonardo promised he would visit you in a dream and put you straight."

"He did and didn't."

"That usually happens when artists dream."

"It was lucid."

"Well, aren't you the lucky dog," Sarah barked. "Lucid is as lucid does. Never mind, it's time to spread your wings and fly," she snapped.

I twisted my neck around and felt my shoulders for wings. "Why? Am I an angel now?"

"Not even close. You're still that white butterfly you just met."

CHAPTER 17 – **DÉJÀ VU AGAIN**

"Man has much power of discourse
which for the most part is vain and false.
Animals have but little, but it is useful and true,
and a small truth is better than a great lie."

Leonardo da Vinci

It was early morning when Sarah and I reached Verrocchio's studio.

The city of Florence was welcoming the first artist of the morning – the divine light. It blessed the narrow streets of Sant' Ambrogio, and inside the workshop on the Via Ghibellina, the miracle of it filled the stale air with gold dust. It brushed every corner and painted the edges of the long tables. It kissed the lips of the water jars and stroked the portraits of goddesses and saints to life.

The senior artists dreamed on, aligned to the business of art. The giant copper sphere awaiting the rooftop of Santa Maria del Fiore was still under construction. It rested low to the ground in a cradle of sticks that made it look like a blank globe, eight feet in diameter.

The metal workers had engineered a small hollow planet with an oculus that looked to me like a Hobbit's front door.

Soon it would rise to crown the cupola of the cathedral's dome - a floating gazebo, hooked on a spire – to become the default image of the Florentine skyline. The burnished orb, seen from below like a copper pearl eclipsing the sun.

A crew of women arrived first to prep the studio. Their tired faces hustled past the paintings of holy families and angels, sweeping the floors with sleepy brooms and the hems of their long skirts. The creative insignificant sisters, daughters, and wives prepared the workshop for their menfolk with raw hands stained saffron and crimson and blue.

I watched the replay of what had been. I wanted to hug Vespers waiting obediently beside her quota of rats, nose twitching, front legs impatiently pawing in anticipation of the breakfast she'd earned.

By the time Vespers reached her bed, an old woman was already beating cornmeal into a bright pudding. Another stirred cilantro into a fresh cauldron of minestrone. The aromas of an awakening kitchen chased away the oppressive night odors and clashed with the more pungent cooking necessary for art: bowls of stewed aloes, egg yolks for tempera, oils of linseed and walnut, distilled pine resin, and foul pots of simmering rabbit-skins for glue.

The glow of white-hot charcoal turned a firing of Madonna figurines terracotta. They stood in submissive rows of blazing martyrdom – sanctified by fire – icons transcending clay and glaze to rise above something finer than mud and water. They endured the fiery torture to become more durable, yet their purpose was to remain the fragile spiritual recipients of human troubles.

The main workroom thawed as the great furnace was stoked twice more to birth its obedient sisterhood of holy mothers.

Ghost laws being somewhat obscure, I didn't know if my vision quest rendered me visible or audible so, I tried to be quiet lest my presence shatter the intimacy of the perfect union Leonardo and I had shared as teenagers. I needn't have worried. It unfolded in technicolor as true thunderbolt Déjà vu.

The previous evening, carpenters had set up the half-finished poplar panel in a new location. Beside it, the cartoon for the 'Tobias' lay unrolled on the workbench weighted down with pottery angels.

Leonardo had arrived early. I recognized the stunning youth from the spotless rose tunic he wore in my old dream.

Vespers was half born on a touch-dry landscape – a charcoal outline, transferred from a red chalk drawing.

Leonardo frowned before the painting, absorbed in thought, arms folded, drumming his fingers against immaculate velvet sleeves. I thought he was listening intently to the whimpers of a dog-sprite begging to be born. But I had clearly startled him because his back straightened when I coughed.

"Cara," he said aloud to the room, "Is that you?"

"You are here," Sarah growled to me. "Everything is as it was.

Please remain quiet as a mouse. My master must work in silence, yes?"

Leonardo glanced in my direction; his eyes unfocused.

"You are still only a misty shape to him."

"Ah, there you are," Leonardo whispered. "I thought it was you."

"Dreams can come true, Cara," Leonardo said without turning his head. "Wait for me."

Earlier, when he'd been alone with the white panel, Leonardo took a stylus and scratched the outlines where Vesper would emerge. He waited impatiently for a week while an unschooled team of ruffians painted the rocks and grass.

By nightfall of the fifth day, the surface was touch dry but unstable. Leonardo prepared a cup of yellow ochre pigment thinned with olive oil, picked up a brush, and looked over his shoulder, bracing himself for a harsh word. But I was the only one there to witness Vesper's birth... and so I watched her emerge, first as a pale grey outline and then filled out with swirls of creamy paint from Naples Yellow to purest lead white.

She took no time at all. Leonardo worked fast. Vesper had been gestating in his mind and on the pages of his notebook for months. Her furry curls materialized in quick decisive movements. Thin black lines picked out her shadows and nose and soon a pair of olive black eyes stared out shining and new into a Florentine evening.

After Vespers had manifested effortlessly, and while his brush was loaded with burnt sienna, Leonardo unconsciously added a deft movement of color that softened an escaped curl at Tobias's temple with a thin glaze of light.

Vespers appeared from her banishment and for a tender moment, a boy and a dog spent a golden hour alone. Leonardo steeled himself to face the overseer, hiding Vespers under his cloak. "That creature belongs in a cage," the overseer said. She might have served as a model for the Tobias but now she's a ratter. Please don't encourage her with food."

Leonardo sent him a look of sadness I knew well. It was then I knew who Leonardo reminded me of.

"Brava," Sarah said. "It's about time."

"Michael," I said and burst into tears, heartbroken.

I was inconsolable until Sarah yiped. "Now stop that grieving nonsense. Strive to be happy. Death is a beginning, and in case you hadn't noticed you're young and pain free – a teenager. Goodness, you're hard to please."

I stood shamefaced in my thin nightgown, distraught, ashamed, and shivering. But to my delight, I noticed my ankles were no longer swollen and my bare feet were delicately shaped – free of bunions. My toes and fingers were slender and smooth.

I sensed Sarah's energy shift to alert and felt her growl inside me as she broke ranks to dive for a mouse scuttling across the floor. She gave a vicious snarl, snapped the neck of her prey in one swift shake, and returned to my side as if nothing had happened. "By the way," she asked casually, "who was that wicked astrologer girl who read your chart? I can't imagine why, but hunting rats always makes me think of her."

"Everyone called her Tari. Her full Greek name was too difficult to pronounce. She had a crush on Michael."

"And?"

"And Nothing. Michael and I were meant to be."

"Until a jealous Tari intervened. So much for puppy love."

"You think she was lying?"

"I don't think; I know. I saw her shadowing you. I heard her thoughts, but it wasn't in my power to intervene. I tried barking to warn you, but your desire for Michael was too loud for you to hear me. The girl was unconscionable. She knew precisely what she was doing."

It was time I asked a question that had been haunting me. "Sarah, if you were at Findhorn, why did I never see or hear you? I don't understand. Couldn't you have spared us all the drama?"

"I was visible and audible, in disguise for a reason. But you didn't have the awareness to see me."

"That surprises me. I thought Findhorn was a period of spiritual awakening for me. You're saying I was unconscious at the time."

"You were riding a wave of sexual infatuation… Michael was

a heady distraction. You were operating within a natural substratum of subconscious endorphins."

Tari's chart clearly revealed the love of my life would die. It declared it several times. She made a point of going over it in detail. All I saw was a confusion of mathematical calculations and geometric angles, showing varying degrees of separation.

Tari pointed to the configurations of symbols crisscrossed with red lines that indicated especially dire predictions. "Here," she said. "And look…" she stabbed the chart. "Here as well." She drew an inward breath and clamped her hands over her mouth in a somewhat theatrical gesture. "*Accht*. I'm so sorry, Stella. There is no doubt."

I paused, remembering. "Michael had called her self-professing prophesies… fears chiseled in stone."

Tari ran the results through the Tarot. The cards confirmed the worst. "There can be no other interpretation," she said looking professional. "Michael will perish in a violent accident. Only you can save him." She fluttered her fingers over the chart. "That line intersecting these houses means the disastrous death of a beloved. If you truly love Michael, you must let him go."

Sarah hopped on two legs and pawed my nightgown. "And you sacrificed Findhorn as penance because you wanted to suffer as much as possible."

"There was no reason to stay in Findhorn without Michael. I

didn't have the heart for living there without him."

"Why are humans so self-destructive. Why do you persist in complicating love when there's so much to be thankful for?"

Leonardo took a step towards the painting.

For a moment I saw Michael in his place. "Michael?"

Leonardo opened his mind. "Stella. *Buona Sera amore mio.*"

Sarah danced a figure eight around us. "Stella," she said gently. "Leonardo WAS your Michael! Michael fell in love with you in the gallery. Leonardo fell in love with you in the lucid dream you shared. You fell in love with Findhorn when you responded to its sound vibration. Leonardo told you he would find you, and then, he did."

"But I saved Michael's life, didn't I?"

Sarah's grunt was that of a scold. "Michael tried to save *yours*. Reincarnation is a many splendored opportunity. Michael is a master."

"Michael always said that timing was everything."

"It is. But sometimes it takes 500 years of astrological time for star-crossed lovers to realign."

"To sleep,
Perchance to dream—
Ay, there's the rub,
For in that sleep of death
What dreams may come."

William Shakespeare

In my old dream, the unfinished 'Tobias' had been propped on a stand, closely attended by a slim teenager with long chestnut hair. Leonardo's palpable energy filled the studio with the aura of a church: the easel an altar, and the young man before it – a devout artist deferring to an icon. He stared through the panel – a slave to its voice. We'd both heard excited barking.

Leonardo turned to me and winked causing thunderbolt butterflies to jumpstart my heart. Only then did I understand how the recently deceased were only a single heartbeat from life.

Sarah jumped into Leonardo's lap and licked his face. "Girls," he declared burying his face in her fur. "You want everything, no."

Sarah rolled in the dust, showing off. "You called the fish the marionette fish when you faced the 'Tobias' as an art student," she said. "By your reckoning, the painting's many weaknesses served to project a young whiz-kid's visions forward like gems sparkling from a handful of pebbles.

The composition was a sprawling shape. Abrasive. Not Leonardo's choice. He preferred triangles. It set him on edge, but he coped by isolating his two contributions. His eyes, once locked onto painting the scales of a single trout, examined the space where a high-spirited mongrel had chosen to materialize. Leonardo, determined to experiment with the new technique of oils, had neglected to inform the overseer. No-one knew but me that the little terrier would evaporate over time and become a ghost dog.

The conflicting styles of seven painters inflicted discord in Leonardo's mind. There were too many flaws to correct: the angel's wings looked too solid to flap. The apprentice, Bartolomeo, had copied a heavy wood and leather contraption made for a pageant, too literally. Fillepe had painted the tassel on Tobias's belt so that it flew free and tangled into a tree on the horizon which destroyed the illusion of distance, the most junior of Andrea's pupils had made.

Sarah stared at me. "You described the rocks as hard poached eggs with insect legs. That was when your eye was true. When you had an eye for details."

"Did I? Leonardo excused his master's figures. He explained that Verrocchio saw figures as carved from marble. But the confraternity paid extra for his experience, and he dutifully suffered through painting when his mind was busy engineering the logistics of hoisting the cathedral's copper sphere into place."

Sarah scratched her back wriggling over the floor, suddenly twisted upright, and rested her chin on her paws. "I *was* there," she growled.

CHAPTER 19 – **CLEAR-SIGHTED**

"Here is my secret. It's quite simple:
One sees *clearly only with the heart.*
Anything essential is invisible to the eyes."

from 'The Little Prince'
Antoine de Saint-Exupéry

Leonardo spoke as a teacher would to a student. "Stella, please note the disturbing left leg of the boy, Tobias. See how it twists back, painfully deformed, but those defects must be overlooked to hear the moral of the story."

Leonardo's voice calmed me. Like Michael, he knew the subtle art of distraction.

"Little could be done to animate the stiff figures," Leonardo continued. "Or save the botched clouds. Master Verrocchio was a sculptor first and a painter by necessity. His painted figures were creatures made of marble with claw-like affectations of twisted fingers who wore colorful clothes to distract the eye from imperfections."

"Master," Sarah interrupted. "I brought Stella as you ordered."
Leonardo ignored Sarah and kept up his critique. "Draperies of stone defy the wind and pin them to the earth, yet the angel, Raphael, come to Earth, makes no contact with the road at all. Do you see it?"

"You sound like my friend, Michael," I said.

Leonardo sent me a crooked smile. "Who is this, Michael? Is

he an angel? Should I be jealous?"

He taught me a lot about art.

"Ahh." He sighed. "So, you were his apprentice, yes?"

The studio filled with sfumato. Leonardo, engulfed by mist, drifted towards the horizon.

"Don't go," I shouted. "Stella, stop him. Can he see us?"

"He senses us which is far more meaningful. We are witnessing what was. He knows you're here. He's conversing with you between the lines of art. He is a master at this. He's never forgotten your dream. He's aware of our presence but his mind is elsewhere. He's already visualizing how to incorporate this optical illusion in a portrait he won't paint for thirty-four years."

Leonardo faded into a blinding white cloud.

"Did I do something to upset him? I can't see him for the light. What's happening? I want to see more. I've waited my entire life to be here. Leonardo promised he would never leave me."

"And he never has. My master always keeps his word. Be patient and all will be revealed."

Silence.

Sarah shook her fur and cleared her throat like a teacher about to give a lecture. "What will appear next is different. It's what-is."

"You mean now in my afterlife experience?"

"A bit crude but ultimately, yes. You are passing through the transitional state of limbo – an ironically imprecise conundrum, that places you precisely in the here and now. It is your personal point of view. Be prepared. You are a human transmitter tuned receiver. All angels are messengers. You are here to view your past."

I turned away. "There's no point in looking back. Nothing can change the past."

"Agreed," Sarah sniffed. "But in rare cases, there are artists who can co-create a future."

"The archangel Raphael heals people's minds, spirits, and bodies; the archangel Michael is the patron saint of the sick, doctors, and paramedics."

"Tari was no angel."

"Her full name was Tarichaea – the Greek name for preserving fish. Rather apt is it not. The universe loves puns."

"How long ago did I die?"

Stella licked my bare toes. "You're still dying, Stella. It's a process that can't be rushed, and as such it's important you understand that events in your life are dovetailed by an order beyond chance. Someone has died several times to be with you. Can you not guess who?"

"Please. No more. I want to go, now. I'm done. Point me in the direction of heaven and I'll *feel* myself there."

"Sorry. You aren't done until I say so. Like it or not. It is the right time to reveal the story I promised."

"Sarah, my nerves are getting the better of me," I said. "I appreciate your diligence, but I need a moment alone to process this being dead, thing. It's somewhat of a shock when death happens without a warning. It's not an instant transition."

"Nothing could be more instantaneous," Sarah replied peevishly in her mind.

I picked up a stick at my feet, glowing with life, and pitched it over her head uttering the word I assumed was music to all dogs' ears. "Fetch!" But Sarah's attention never wavered. Her black button eyes stayed calmly locked on mine.

Naturally, I looked away first.

"Oh, Stella," she chirped. "You noodle. What do you think I've been doing this whole time?"

"I don't understand."

Sarah shook dust and leaves from her fur and made a chuffing sound in her throat I can only assume was chuckling. "I AM A FETCH!"

"I still don't…"

"A fetch is an OMEN - an apparition that appears before an impending death."

"Yes, and I wrote in my journal that my *eyes* were dying. But surely, I didn't have to fully die. That seems a tad, pardon the expression, overkill."

Sarah tilted her head. "You DECLARED your eyes were dying which is an entirely different fish," she howled. "As I recall, you fervently offered it up to the night sky with heartfelt conviction. The universe couldn't help but respond in kind. Power begets power."

The light faded from the stick, now magically returned to my feet.

"I am your fetch," Sarah said bowing her head. "I am your heart."

CHAPTER 20 – **SARAH'S SECRET**

from 'The Little Prince'
Antoine de Saint-Exupéry

For once. I was annoyed with Sarah. "I believe this is my time to rest in peace. I don't want to guess. Whatever happened is over. It's too late for second guessing. I'm tired."

"Pretend for a doggone minute that I am a scientist," Sarah said miffed. "Can you *do* that? Can you do that for Leonardo, or Michael, or me? Can you *do* that for yourself?"

I sent her a look of pure loathing. "A white butterfly can do anything," I said.

"Leonardo's presence is also Michael's. Not shared, but implicitly, they are of one soul-mind. Did you actually believe I could speak in human language? Stella, my angel, all your inner voices: your subconscious muses, mirror reflections, inner guidance, Madame Universe, the fish, Leonardo's, Raphael's, and mine, were Michael's. I've been with him a long time."

"I need to speak with Michael. Now! When did he die?"

"The first time he passed was May 2, 1512. Ring any bells?"

"That's…"

"Yes. My master, Leonardo, died May 2, 1512. What does that tell you?"

"That all this time, it was Michael? Was he Leonardo?"

"A master is always a master. Leonardo reincarnated as Michael to be with you. He's a patient soul. Stubborn, of course. He had to be. Determined as a mastermind requires. You only heard Leonardo's voice after you'd been thinking about Michael."

"Now that's where you're wrong. After Findhorn, there were times Leonardo popped in for a chat."

"That's because Michael was thinking of *you*. The two of you are always connected. He warned and pleaded with you but in the end, he got out of your way. He suffered terribly. Letting you go was an act of selfless courage. On the worst days he relied on me. That's where I beetled off to when I disappeared. I was with Michael in Scotland. But he put his trust in time. In times long passed and in *you*."

"Where is he now. Can I go to him?"

"He's waiting nearby."

"But his death could be years away."

"Not to worry, time flies in the afterlife. He will arrive shortly."

"Is that supposed to calm me? I am terrified."

"Don't be," two voices said in unison. A pair of teenagers emerged from the light. Leonardo and Michael Grant stood side-by-side. Vespers' ghostly form trotted through them and sat at their feet. Michael smiled; arms outstretched. "Remember me," he said grinning a lopsided smile.

Seeing double was a shock but I believe Michael's smile marked the precise moment of my death because I felt a freedom within me inseparable from remorse. I apologized rather feebly. "Michael, I should have stayed with you. But it's becoming clear that some part of me must have needed to leave you. Please forgive me."

Michael shrugged gallantly. "Your fear eclipsed your right to be happy, that's all. It happens all the time. There's nothing new under the stars. The adage 'love is blind' stems from feeling unworthy."

"So, Raphael was right?"

"Not quite. Give credit where credit's due," he said reaching down to pet Vespers. "A dog will always tell you truths that will eventually save you. You wanted to save me. And now, you must forgive Tari so she can move on."

"Done."

"Then come here. I'm tired of waiting."

"Who? I mean, which one of you?"

Vespers disappeared. Light flickered between Michael and

Leonardo's forms like a lantern in a storm, finally settling on Michael. "I am the culmination," Michael said stepping forward. "Leonardo is me as I am him."

"And what of Keats' theory of anonymity?"

"Keats was a deeply depressed poet fighting against dying young. He'd lost his belief in immortality. But he was essentially correct. "Humans are signatures writ in water, eternally here and not here, now and forever."

THE DENOUEMENT
DOGMATIC TO THE END

*"The greatest fear a dog knows
is that you won't come back
when you go out the door."*

Fifteenth-century Florence, the birthplace of fine art, cradle of poetry, music, and literature, was infested with vermin.

Artists workshops prospered along the Via Ghibellina but none were as profitable nor required the services of a skilled rat catcher more than the studio of Andrea Verrocchio, master sculptor and architect turned entrepreneur.

Vespers, a common terrier, and natural ratter, performed a nightly killing spree for a roof over her head, a bowl of bread scraps drizzled with leftover soup, and a warm sleeping place during the day. Human kindness, as yet unknown to her, she neither sought nor missed.

Hiding in plain sight was never an option. To keep her place, Vespers needed only to follow three simple rules: kill every rodent in sight, avoid the eyes of the overseer, and become invisible when the morning came because a small working-dog underfoot on an overcrowded production floor is a tripping disaster waiting to happen.

In her second month of life, Vespers had been roughly spirited away, dognapped from a bed of sweet-scented farm straw, and traded to a passing tinker on his way to Florence.

Cruelly, after separation from her litter, it transpired, there had been no trees or grassy meadows in Vespers' puppyhood.

"Natural ratters," the tinker had proclaimed holding Vespers up for inspection, praising the virtues of the common terrier. "Don't let her scrawny looks fool you. She's fearless... A trained voracious hunter... Better than a dozen cats!" And so, within an hour inside the city gates, Vespers was exchanged for a crust of bread to the overseer of Andrea Verrocchio's bottega and bundled off to the life of a working dog.

Every evening, undercover of darkness a battle raged between animal warriors until every mouse and rat was slain. Vespers dispatched them with ease, dumped their limp corpses into a corner, and waited patiently for dawn when the women artists arrived to prepare the studio and her breakfast.

The afternoon that Vespers left her cozy sleeping nest hadn't been Vespers' idea. She had been procured against her will by a pair of hands. But the hands were gentle, and she restrained her instinct to struggle. Once befriended, Vespers the night rat catcher, had a compelling reason to risk injury, a beating, or being exiled to the streets. Loving kindness eclipsed the dangers of being detected out of bounds.

There was no turning back after finding her master. But when

Leonardo vanished her grief was unbearable. Vespers, adopted, cherished, and orphaned in the space of a single glorious week posing as a lapdog, was frantic. There was no way of understanding her master's absence was temporary. Her protector was gone. Vespers searched for him everywhere. But staying silent under pressure was not in her nature. She yelped and barked her way onto the floor of chaos, snapping and snarling.

Crossing a factory floor in daylight was a hazardous obstacle course for a high-spirited terrier designed low to the ground.

Vespers' destination of care and compassion was a beeline through the worst of it, jostled in a crush of *head-in-the-cloud* painters, carpenters, metal workers, and kiln loaders – a battlefield of blind feet and indifferent wheels.

A sea of angry faces wavered from above. Paint and plaster dripped from her sky. Walls of human voices blocked her north and south; abrasive colors eclipsed her east and west. Accidently being squashed to death was almost guaranteed by her small size.

Sadly, in an instinctive reaction to pain, Vespers nipped the overseer's ankle for stepping on her toes.

Vespers underfoot swiftly became Vespers outside.

Once banished, inclement weather and the horrors of the marketplace vied with horses' hooves, cartwheels, and slavering streetwise curs fighting to the death over rancid scraps of offal and bones. Vespers, herself a mere scrap of insignificant meat, was a tasty morsel in a dog-eat-dog survival contest.

She slunk from door to door, up and down streets, exploring alleyways until she came to a city gate. Beyond it were rolling green hills and swaying trees. But feeling unworthy of such pleasures, she humbly turned back.

Vespers huddled on the studio's doorstep where she sniffed the shoes of every passerby for the familiar scent of her beloved master. But in her concentration, she failed to lift her gaze to an approaching wagonload of marble.

Transparent as air, Vespers slipped through the studio's oak door and assumed a vigil under her master's worktable. She was free. And when her master returned, her joy was complete.

500 years later, near the sacred precincts of London's Trafalgar Square, in the hushed rat-free halls of The National Gallery, Vespers materialized after hearing a tour guide utter her favorite word sound. A word she knew by heart. The word, Leonardo, made her ears perk up and her tail twitch madly. She waited impatiently, suppressing her need to howl down the moon.

And when the doors were locked at 6 p.m. sharp, and the visiting tourists headed for the theatre district, the night life inside the gallery began.

Security guards making their rounds, never guessed a feisty white terrier intent on invisibility, followed them at a safe distance, having learned the heartless nature of men with cruel boots.

Vespers was on the prowl, sniffing out the heady scent of loving affection, on a mission to find a lost Leonardo. Not one of his masterpieces but *her* master, friend, and partner in art.

Her nightly cries set the security cameras beeping. And after a lowbrow tabloid ran the banner headline: 'NATIONAL GALLERY SECURITY GUARD… PSYCHIC or BARKING MAD?', folks normally blind to the finer points of fine art suddenly felt an irresistible urge to wander the rarified corridors of culture on a quest for a spirit dog.

Londoners love a mystery and if a ghost is involved or even the hint of a haunt is dropped, reporters desperate for a story angle converge on it like white butterflies to a beach. Ghostly sightings or *'hearings'* of a phantom dog never fail to revive curiosity in the afterlife or sell newspapers.

Busloads of tourists flocked to London WC2N 5DN to mill about the gallery's famous steps for group tours. The hottest ticket in town was a cultural fast track to the Sainsbury Wing, decked out with heat sensitive cameras, night goggles, tape recorders, and high frequency ultrasonic dog whistles.

WILLIAM SHAKESPEARE

'STARRY NIGHT' - Vincent van Gogh, 1889

V Knox writes cozy 'metaphysical' novels for discriminating bookworms who savor reading long strange books as slowly as possible. Her invented genres of choice are 'Cozy Outer Limits' and 'Art History Delivered in a Ghost Story'.

Veronica obtained a Fine Arts degree from the University of Alberta where she developed an imaginative take on art history that led to an untapped source for stories. She discovered that inanimate objects were rarely bereft of life and that paintings have juicy secrets to tell.

She explores the creative inner worlds of autistic savants and master artists, and in one case, the unknown child in the Titanic cemetery. She explores the discrepancies between reality and lucid dreams, fishes the depths of the subconscious, the afterlife, reincarnation, the anomalies of parallel lives and dimensions, the classic psyche of 'the ghostly lover', reconciles historical facts with surreal fiction, and has written fourteen 'outer limits' novels.

Veronica remains intent on listening to the ethereal echoes from objects in museums and the voices of the Italian Renaissance – the artists as well as their anonymous subjects and companions. She grants them second chances to air their grievances, tell their stories, and together they set the dreariest history books on fire.

other books 
by Veronica Knox

Cozy 'Outer Limits', Art History Mysteries, and Time-Slip magical realism

'DISAPP'EARRING TWICE' – Aurelia Marcus, an aging eccentric shadowed by the spirit of a girl from a famous painting, rents a castle by the sea to write a novel before she forgets the story she feels compelled to write based on her recurring dreams of a past life.
AURELIA MARCUS DISAPPEARED LONG BEFORE SHE RAN AWAY FROM HOME

'ADORATION – Loving Botticelli' – The romance between a retired art history professor and a five-hundred-year-old portrait leads from obsession to seduction.
LIFE CAN BE AN IMMORTAL COMEDY

'WOO WOO – the posthumous love story of Miss Emily Carr' – the artist Emily Carr, an eccentric spinster, comes to her senses sixty-seven years after her death and calls down the energy of her animal totem, Woo the monkey, to rekindle the love of a rejected suitor – *a fanciful homage to Emily Carr inspired by her memoirs.*

'THE UNTHINKABLE SHOES' – *a story of reincarnation and extraordinary sacrifice inspired by a museum exhibit of child's shoes from the Titanic.* When death separates two children on the Titanic who were destined to marry, the barefoot ghost of the boy chooses to remain earthbound as the surviving girl's invisible childhood companion. Finding a pair of lost shoes is their one chance to stay together.
A 'LOST BOY' FROM TITANIC LOSES HIS SHOES BETWEEN HEAVEN AND THE DEEP BLUE SEA

'THE INDIGO PEARL' – *a story of YOUNG LOVE & OLD SOULS - *book one of two:* When the consciousness of Delphi Sharpe, an autistic woman with the extrasensory ability to converse with paintings and birds, is transplanted into the circuits of an android programmed to retrieve famous works of art lost in the distant past, intelligence is no longer artificial. Delphi must fight her way back to love, one pearl at a time.
AI = AUTISTIC INTELLIGENCE – 'STATE OF THE ART' TIME TRAVEL JUST BECAME TRANSCENDENTAL

'PEARL BY PEARL' – *a story of YOUNG LOVE & OLD SOULS - *book two of two:* Two rivalling 'art whisperers' become single-mindedly obsessed to consummate the love of Delphi's life – a teenage boy in a 500-year-old portrait. But while the spirit of Delphi wants to rest in peace with her beloved, her counterpart intends to exact revenge on the art syndicate that exploited them.
SOMETIMES IT TAKES TWO LIVES TO MAKE ONE WOMAN

'I WAS THERE' – the art of time travel in a 15th century dreamscape poem

THE BEDE SERIES: – GHOSTS WHO INVITE READERS TO COME ALIVE!

'**TWINTER – the first portal**' – a magical realism time-slip adventure *book one of 'The Bede Series':* Bede Hall, an abandoned and disgruntled stately home, is desperate. It must rally its dispersed family before it's sold to developers. Its new residents, a pair of thirteen-year-old twins, seek out a girl lost in time whose apparition has haunted the estate for generations, but meeting her opens a time portal that reveals a terrible secret. In order to rescue her and protect the future, the teens form a team of otherworldly allies called the 'Twinters'.
BEDE HALL IS ALIVE, BUT ALL IS NOT WELL

'**TIME FALLS LIKE SNOW**' – a magical realism time-slip adventure *book two of 'The Bede Series':* The secrets of Bede Hall's timely past continue with the sixteen-year-old twins working in league with a team of ghosts and 'twice-borns' who have been monitoring Bede's secrets for hundreds of years. It falls to the rules of twindom, the Great Sphinx of Egypt, and a colony of mystical cats to save the future. THE 'TWINTERS' ARE RUNNING OUT OF TIME IN A LANDSCAPE WHERE HISTORY IS POSITIVELY ANCESTRAL

'**TOMORROW AGAIN**' – a magical realism time-slip adventure *book three of four in 'The Bede Series':* To save Bede Hall, a disgruntled stately home nestled against Hadrian's Wall in England, a pair of telepathic twins, at odds over logic and metaphysics, must fulfill an ancient prophecy, and rescue its resident ghost. But sending them to ancient Egypt, Pangea, and Mars turns out to be the shortest route to saving the planet from a nuclear winter.

'**SNOW BEHIND THE DOOR**' – documents the *time-slipped* memories of the abandoned ghost-child of Bede Hall, named

Snow, in search of the family she glimpses in dreams and the dusty mirrors of a stately home that has sheltered earth's time portals, guarded by an ancient line of royal Egyptian cats for thousands of years.

THE MEMOIR OF A CHILD GHOST WITH AMNESIA

acknowledgments

I am grateful to my spiritual teacher, Eckhart Tolle.
His insights have inspired my conscious storytelling in 14
novels from a middle-grade time-slip series to ghost stories
where ghosts are a metaphor
for lost humans making their way home.
I am grateful to Max Ehrmann for his poem 'Desiderata',
And to the emperor Marcus Aurelius for his wise counsel.
I am grateful for lucid dreams,
the latest muse on my shoulder,
my imaginary friend and mentor, Leonardo,
and thank my lucky stars
for my loyal dogs Ginger and Peyton

If you enjoyed this novella
please spread the word.
Thank you.

Veronica Knox - *May 2022*